Shopping for a Billionaire 4

by Julia Kent

A confusing fight, a garbage-covered car, and a mom who shares her past as a "stripper" all drive Shannon to the edge of madness. When her big shot at mystery shopping luxury properties leads to another crazy toilet incident, it's Declan to the rescue...but can they take the "plunge"? The Shopping series from *New York Times* bestselling author Julia Kent reaches its conclusion with heart, heat, and hilarity.

Part 4 of a 4-part series.

Sign up for my New Releases and Sales email list at my blog to get the latest scoop on new eBooks, freebies and more:
http://jkentauthor.blogspot.com/p/sig n-up-for-my-new-releases-email- list.html

Table of Contents

Chapter One...1
Chapter Two..11
Chapter Three...23
Chapter Four...33
Chapter Five...41
Chapter Six..47
Chapter Seven...55
Chapter Eight..67
Chapter Nine...79
Chapter Ten..91
Chapter Eleven..105
Chapter Twelve...113
Chapter Thirteen...125
Chapter Fourteen...133
Chapter Fifteen...141
Chapter Sixteen...153
Chapter Seventeen..169
Chapter Eighteen...181
Chapter Nineteen...191
Chapter Twenty...201
Chapter Twenty-One......................................213
Other Books by Julia Kent...............................217
About the Author..219

Chapter One

Declan's text says:
We'll talk

"That's it?" I gasp, Amanda closing her eyes slowly, as if someone reached over with fingertips and shut them, like on a corpse. It is apt; it feels like someone just died. I'm supposed to hop in the shower and get ready for work, but how do you do that when your entire life is imploding?

"He answered, at least." She reaches in behind the shower curtain and turns on the water for me. A part of me feels infantilized. I can turn on my own damn water. I don't need help. I know how to use a shower.

Another part of me is helpless and racked with a kind of cryogenic emotional freeze that renders me useless. She leaves the room and gently points to the phone.

"Answer back."

The door shuts like her eyelids did just a moment ago, though Chuckles manages to slip in through the inch-sized crack as Amanda leaves. Didn't cats accompany the pharaohs in ancient times as they were laid to rest in their burial crypts?

Something's dying right now, and as he snuggles up against my ankles without meowing, his presence calm and serene, I feel a deep disturbance inside. Chuckles is being nice to me?

This is *bad.*

Tremors fill my fingers as I pick up my phone and stare at his sparse text. Two words. I get two measly words? No replies until now, no acknowledgement of the cyber-mess that has made real life an emotional land mine for me.

Just… *We'll talk.*

I type back:

Okay. See you soon.

I hit Send with fingers vibrating so much they could be used as a sex toy prototype.

By the time I finish going through the motions and cleaning my hair and body, he's had plenty of opportunity to answer.

Nope. No text.

I'm all cried out and numb now, wondering how we could go from talking about finding each other and enjoying so much together to this coldness, this arctic freeze that doesn't even have an explanation. Not even a pseudo-explanation. We're dancing on broken glass and denying that it hurts. Ignoring the river of blood that lubricates the pain. Only maybe I'm the one feeling all the pain. Perhaps this is nothing to him. A blip. I'm someone he used to sleep with and all that's left is the final "It's not you…" conversation where he walks away and I disintegrate into a thousand shards of glass.

That he walks all over with bloody feet.

It's not that I really think he's that cold. In fact, the opposite: the man I have gotten to know over the past month isn't the man who is doing this right now. Two different men. Or—two different sides of the same man? Why do I have this long history of being surprised when people show a different side of themselves?

You would think I'd stop being so naïve, so childlike, being shocked when someone changes. I guess it's because I don't change. I am who I am (whoever that is...) and I'm what Josh calls a WYSIWYG—What You See Is What You Get. No hidden subtext.

Maybe, though, for Declan I'm a WYSINWYW—What You See Is Not What You Want.

I need to pull him aside and call it all out, to say what isn't being said. How do you do that when you don't even know what the other person is thinking? I'm no mind reader. I definitely don't want to be one, either, because *eww*. Can you imagine how quickly you'd learn how perverted everyone in the world really is?

And how judgmental?

I get plenty of perversion and judgment from my mom, thanks. I don't need more. If I get to have a superpower, mind-reading isn't what I want. I'd prefer a clitoris inside my vagina, thank-youverymuch.

Now *that's* a superpower.

Yet when I ask Declan what's going on, I get *we'll talk*? The sudden sub-zero temperature change from him is starting to look like the North Atlantic current being shut down.

Men. Can't live with them, can't shove an

EpiPen in their groin and keep them.

"You ready?" Amanda calls out as I towel off my hair.

"You're still here?"

"I figured I'd drive you to the meeting."

"Because you think I can't drive?"

"Because I think this is going to be hard."

I stew over that one for a second, wondering why everyone thinks I'm a fragile porcelain doll. Then I realize I am. Right now, at least.

"Okay," I call out. "But we're taking your car. If I'm about to be dumped, it won't be while driving the Turdmobile."

"A girl's gotta have standards," she shouts back with a laugh.

* * *

It's an icehouse in here.

And the air conditioning isn't even on.

Unfortunately, Declan never responded to my text message, and he was also not anywhere near the hallway where I lingered like a seventh grader hoping to bump into her crush outside the band room instrument storage closet.

(What? Like you never did that…)

The players are the same, but the game has changed. James and Andrew sit on one side of the table, a glass of water in front of a third, empty chair. Amanda, Greg, and I are on the other side. No tension; James and Greg are in cordial conversation when Amanda and I join them. Greg came first to settle some details, and now the entire show begins.

Without Declan.

Andrew's giving me inscrutable looks. I seriously cannot tell whether he knows about the Jessica Asshat Coffin mess, and if he does, what he thinks. He looks like a slightly darker version of Declan, with the same bone structure, a jaw that can go hard and resolute with anger or firmness as well as it can go soft and sweet with a smile.

But they're both impassive when it comes to expressing emotion in a business setting, and I suspect Andrew's like his dad in that respect as well. James just looks kind of dismayed with the world all the time. Like everyone is going to disappoint him anyhow, so why bother?

As if I said that aloud, the elder McCormick cuts his eyes my way and gives me a long look. His eyes narrow to triangles, so much like Declan's that I feel that strange tightness in my chest. Not anaphylactic shock, but something close to it. I think it's the feeling of having my organs removed from my body by my own stupidity.

Starting with my heart.

James calls the meeting to order. Amanda and I share frantic looks meant to convey one singular question:

Did I sleep with a billionaire in a limo only to have it all ruined by pretending to be gay and running into my ex's mother, who turned to a social media whore in an attempt to reclaim her son's balls?

5

And the answer:

Pretty much.

Time machines are *soooooo* underrated. If I had one and was given one chance to go back in time and fix anything I wanted, I would go back to the moment Greg announced those gay prejudice credit union shops and say *no*.

(Yes, I know I'm supposed to say I'd go back in time and kill Hitler or stop the burning of Joan d'Arc, but I'm kind of shallow right now.)

No time machine. No giant sinkhole to swallow me up. Not even a psychotic cat who can pee on James' foot and give me a reason to escape. Only—

Declan.

He walks into the meeting and gives everyone a gracious smile with frozen eyes so cold you could use them in a camp cooler for a long weekend and still have cold beer.

"I apologize for being late. I was detained."

"You make it sound like you had no choice, son," James says with a low chuckle. Andrew and Declan share a look that reminds me of Amanda and me, minus the lip biting and grimaces.

"It felt like it," Declan growls.

James leans back, clearly in the catbird seat, and it's dick-waving time now. "If you're going to run the entire marketing department for an international corporation, you have to accept that some cultures handle the standard business lunch quite differently." He shoots Greg a knowing wink.

Greg winks back like a drag queen with a stuck

eyelash. "Quite differently." He's trying to fit in, and I know that, but my sympathy lies with the women whose faces are pressed flat against the corporate glass ceiling, with a stripper's pastie-covered nipples smashed on the other side of the glass as we all try to pretend there's nothing to see here, folks.

"Is this 'business lunch' an issue that all marketing professionals need to deal with?" I keep my voice as even as possible, but even I detect the officiousness in it. Amanda gives me a sharp look, while Greg rubs his mouth like there's something in there. His foot, maybe.

Declan's in the middle of pulling files from his briefcase, but as my voice fills the air he moves more slowly, lips twitching. Aha. I nailed it. I'm not jealous—whatever "standard business lunch" and "some cultures" are code for doesn't matter. I'm imagining strippers as a side dish along with sixteen-ounce medium-rare tenderloins and the dripping butter sauce for their lobster being poured over augmented breasts on a stage.

James and Declan share a long look. Declan gives a nudge of his head, in deference or—perhaps —to allow the old man to make a fool of himself.

Either way, it's about to get real.

And it just got a lot colder in here.

"I would say that all vice presidents of marketing who work with a variety of international clients will eventually be taken on a more... salacious expedition at least once or twice in a career." James' cocky smile looks like a caricature of Declan's. "The higher you fly, the greater the lengths you go to please a client and close the deal."

Greg looks a bit sick. *I'm* his closer. What does this mean? Do I need to cultivate a taste for pole dancing?

"What about a female vice president? Would she be expected to attend a…" I bite my words off carefully and spit them out in slow, snappy chunks. "…sa-la-cious 'standard business lunch' experience, which, I assume, means hookers and blow."

Andrew is taking a drink of water and does a spit take like something out of a Jimmy Fallon clip. Most of the water in his mouth lands on Amanda's cleavage across the table, which makes her jump to her feet.

It is so much easier to take on the client's asshattery than to deal with the subtext in the room, and James is giving me fabulous fodder for my self-righteous streak. Way easier than dealing with that tight-chest feeling about losing Declan, who has managed to avoid eye contact with me.

"I hardly think you're in a position to comment on salacity and business relations, Ms. Jacoby." James' eyes are those of a hawk, coming in for the kill. "How *was* that helicopter ride, son?" He doesn't look at Declan. His eyes are entirely on me.

I have a choice as all the oxygen in the room disappears, along with any hope of a relationship with Declan, or of an ongoing career for me in the bigger Boston corporations. I can back off and go home and cry and eat pint after pint of ice cream and suck down Hot 'n Sour soup like it's about to

8

be banned like Sriracha sauce, or I can stand up to the big bad CEO who decided I'm an ant and his words are a magnifying glass in a nice patch of sunlight.

"Dad." One word. Declan's single word is a nuclear bomb. The heat coming from Declan's anger can keep a small village in Greenland warm for the winter.

"Oh, please, Dec. The driver and the pilot told me. It's not as if she's *really* the lesbian that people on that Twiterlicious thing are saying."

Andrew's wiping his face with a handkerchief and offers one to Amanda while giving her a speculative look that I'd normally pay way more attention to, but I'm in the middle of soul death, so I'm kind of distracted. Where's my Mom with a good butt plug story about now? I'd even welcome Agnes and Corrine's nonagenarian cat fights.

"Good play, Ms. Jacoby." He leans forward on the table. "I know from Declan's glowing descriptions of you that you're about as gay as I am poor. That tells me you held on to your assumed identity quite thoroughly so that you could perform the function assigned to you by the client."

"What does that have to do with anything?" Declan's voice could cut diamonds.

"It means she's the perfect candidate for corporate espionage."

Chapter Two

Greg's turn to do a spit take. "Is that business guru speak for mystery shopping these days?"

James laughs. How can the man laugh when he's managed to alienate and/or piss off every person in the room except for Andrew, who appears to be trying to decide whether to be alienated, pissed off, or to ogle Amanda's low-ish-cut silk blouse?

For the record, his penis appears to win.

Family trait.

Wait a minute. James knows I slept with Declan in the limo and in the helicopter, and what the hell, let's throw in the lighthouse part, too. He knows about the credit union mystery shop and me and Amanda. He knows about Jessica's Twittergate mess. What the hell *doesn't* this man know?

"No, Greg. Corporate espionage means I'd like for Ms. Jacoby to be assigned to evaluate The Fort —"

Amanda's sharp intake of horrified breath makes Andrew perk up as her chest lifts.

"—and also Le Chateau."

Now she shrieks. It's a fairly professional-sounding shriek, but still. "Le Chateau is your competitor! Why would she mystery shop—oh…" She closes down to neutral as fast as she ramped up to livid. It's impressive, and I'd appreciate it more if Declan weren't shredding my heart.

Scribbling furiously, her next words come out like machine gun bullets. "By having the same person evaluate both high-end properties, you get an even sense of the failings and mastery in each."

"Indeed. And we need someone who can hold their cover," James says with a cordial tone that makes me question my sanity. Wasn't he just being an asshole? How am I supposed to keep track of the villain in here if he keeps changing his personality?

"*I* held my cover," Amanda mutters. Greg gives her a dirty look. Amanda gives him double back. He blanches.

"Yes, you did," James notes. "And after Shannon successfully finishes both properties, you can be the next evaluator in three months' time. Your own mastery did not go unnoticed."

"But *you're* not really gay, right?" Andrew blurts out, his eyes on Amanda's breasts.

Awkward.

James rolls his eyes. "My sons need to retake their sexual harassment training, I see."

"It's not sexual harassment," Declan and I say in unison.

Oh, thank God. He understands. He understands! I close my eyes and inhale slowly, then open them to give him a big, friendly, warm, loving grin.

He stares back with green ice cubes.

Uh.

"The mess is unconventional, I'll admit,"

James adds, pushing contracts to Greg. "But Ms. Jacoby isn't a known entity in the circles we inhabit —"

Translation: I'm a nobody, so he doesn't have to worry that I'll be recognized at a competitor's luxury property even though Jessica has been tweeting about me to all the cyberspace rubberneckers in Boston.

"—and I trust the evaluations will give us valuable insight into gaining a competitive edge."

"In other words, you're giving me more responsibility, and expanding the contract with Consolidated Evalu-shop?" I ask, and this time it's my eyes that are on Declan while asking James the question.

"Yes," Declan answers me. Not James. "You're very good at living a double life and are quick on your feet when it comes to lying." He cuts his eyes away. "That will suit you well in business."

No. *No no no no no.*

Amanda pivots and coughs, the strain getting to her. Andrew's eyes ping between me, Declan, her chest, and his dad. Greg just looks constipated, eyebrows bunched like a caterpillar in heat as he reviews contracts that have been read so many times they might as well be the Bible.

"And," James adds, stuffing folders into his briefcase, clearly done, "how's business?"

The spear aimed from an icy stretch of glacier that is his heart right now hits its target with pinpoint precision. That's what Jessica tweeted to Declan.

"May I speak with you in the hallway?" I hiss at him, grabbing his forearm. He turns into a marble statue, though emotion flickers in his eyes. His Adam's apple bobs as he swallows, and his stiff muscles radiate mixed signals.

"If you wish." He shakes off my hand, though not with an angry movement. More with a cold precision that somehow is worse.

"We'll finish negotiations," James says, eyes twinkling, as if he's accomplished something. "And it's good to see you walking around, Ms. Jacoby. Last I heard from Declan, you were bed bound."

Another sex joke? Are you kidding me? My tongue loosens in my mouth, ready to lash him, when even the venerable James McCormick has the decency to turn red with embarrassment and backtrack.

"I meant your allergic reaction to the stings. That you were in the hospital. In a hospital bed," he stammers. "My son was very worried."

"Your son was the only reason I'm here," I say gently. The amusement is gone from his expression, replaced by a kind of sad intrigue, his body uptight and loose at the same time as if it can't make up its mind.

But control and authority prevail as his mask reappears and he turns away from me with a dismissive wave. "I'm glad Declan could do what he needed to do in a crisis. That proves he's matured."

Andrew's neck snaps toward his dad, a red fury pouring into his skin so fast it seems he'll

14

burst. I turn toward Declan to find him in the threshold, one hand curled into a gripping claw on the door's trim, close to snapping the wood in half.

What the hell is going on? This conversation suddenly has nothing to do with me and Declan, or with Twitterhead Coffin, or with my credit union shop. There's a subtext here I don't understand, and it stings.

Declan lets go of the door with a loud smack of his palm against the wood and slowly, with a little too much control, moves out. I can't even admire the undulating grace of his anger or ask him why he and his dad are speaking in Angry Man Code, a language that seems designed to neuter the other man and stuff his balls down his throat.

But this isn't just macho bullcrap. James' comment about Declan and crises and maturing resonates somewhere inside Declan, but he's wound so tight, and I'm skating on thin ice already.

There's no way to be open and just ask what's going on.

He spins around so abruptly that I stagger and fall against the wall, banging my hip on a piece of trim. "What do we need to discuss?"

How could the same man who told me I was beautiful, who put his mouth in places where only speculums have gone, look at me like I'm a gnat that should be swatted out of existence?

"Can we have coffee and talk?" I can't think of what else to say.

He just blinks. No answer. I stare back, unyielding, even as my mind screams in childlike sadness. Something is broken, and it's not just me. I didn't break it. He's not telling me something and it's between us, without shape or form, taking up all the known room, and yet it has no name.

"Coffee?" He makes a strangled huffing sound. "How about at one of my stores?" His voice is acid. "I hear we're testing a new peppermint mocha with wasabi syrup. Oh, wait—you would know better than I do."

I actually flinch and pull back as if he's slapped me. If he had, it would be easier. "I-I-I just want to talk. About the pretending to be gay thing, and the Jessica Coffin thing, and—"

"I know you're not gay." His voice carries a bit as he punches that sentence out with a tongue made of steel, his face so tight you could turn it into a drum.

"I guessed as much. It shouldn't have been hard to figure out."

He makes a sour face and glances at an imaginary watch he isn't wearing. Either he really does have another meeting or he's in a hurry to be done with me, and the latter feels like ice picks in my gut.

"Shannon, I don't know what your game is. Maybe the other night was all acting—"

"No! I swear! No game!" An ominous layer of straight-up terror begins to cover me like a blanket that brings no comfort.

"You're paid to act," he says viciously. "*Act*. You're paid to pretend, right? To go into a business setting and pretend to be something you aren't, all

16

while observing every nuance, every detail. You're a chameleon who changes to meet the expectations of the people in that setting, with the ruthless efficiency of an international spy." His breath is heavy and full of anger. "You're quite proud of it."

"But not with *you*," I plead. "Never with you."

"How am I supposed to know? You're a bit like the boy who cried wolf, honey."

My head ricochets back. Honey. That's what he called me in the hospital.

"You told that blowhard's mother you're just dating me to close a deal. Well, you did." He motions toward the closed door. "My dad just gave you a plum new assignment. Your company makes more money, we get a crack corporate spy, and everyone goes home happy and satisfied."

He's baring his teeth now in a smile that is so ferociously barren of compassion or caring that it mesmerizes me. I can't turn away, but at the same time I want to curl up into a ball and cry.

"You really think that about me?" I whisper quietly. Mercifully, the tears are behind a wall of summoned self-righteousness. I need it right now. I know every word he says is dead on in its own twisted way, but I can't let it be true, because there's a larger Truth with a capital T right next to his smaller truth.

"What else am I supposed to think? You told me yourself in the lighthouse that you're 'shopping for a billionaire.' You told your ex-boyfriend's mother that you're dating me to close a business deal, and some screwed-up game of grown-up telephone ends on Twitter with a high-society wannabe trying to embarrass me on a social media platform so silly it uses bird metaphors."

I snort nervously.

Pity fills his eyes. Oh, no. This is end game. I know this look, because it's the same expression Steve had when he dumped me. *No. No. No.*

"I can't do this, Shannon."

No. Please.

"You're just too…much."

Great. So he lied to me about loving my abundant body.

"Too many layers to tease through, too many what-ifs, too many half-truths and un-truths—"

Wait! He's not slamming my curves. He's slamming my integrity! Hold on there, buddy. You can make fun of my fat (which he didn't), but—

"That is bull," I thunder back. A receptionist at a desk at the end of the hall cranes her neck forward, peering at us. Like a turtle, she snaps it back, hidden.

When Steve dumped me I just sniffled and took it, curled into myself on a park bench near my apartment, sitting on the lawn of a local college. No way am I cowering now. If this is over, it'll be over on my terms. Or, at least, I won't go down without a defense. A fight.

Words.

"There's bull here, all right." He's breathing hard, and if this were a sitcom or a Nora Ephron movie this is the part where we'd shout at each other and then he'd grab my face, hard, and kiss me like I've never been kissed before, until my muffled protests are drained out of me by the sudden clarity that only hot lips can provide.

"You spend your life trying to get everyone else to believe you're something you're not, Shannon. And when you're not play-acting, you're begging for validation. You change yourself to become whatever it is you think everyone wants you to be." He runs an angry hand through his thick hair, the dark waves spreading across his forehead as pained eyes finally show me a tiny bit of the tempest inside him.

A mail clerk trundles by with a squeaky cart. We're blocking the hall. He stops and waits, staring dumbly at us, one finger in the air like he's about to interrupt in the geekiest way possible. He reminds me of Mark J., and that? THAT fact is the one that makes the tears almost pour out, because it reminds me of the day I met Declan, of how Mr. Sex in a Suit looked that morning, so crisp and unknown, and how in the short expanse of one month I could go from hot, liquid lust for a guy I don't know to this.

Arguing in a hallway at work about whether I'm sincere or not.

"You don't know me." It's the only sentence I can form right now.

"You didn't give me a chance! I took a chance on you, and you just—" Some primal emotion without name blinds me. "Which Shannon am I supposed to date—the one lying in the men's room, the one lying at the credit union, the one lying about her allergy?" His voice breaks.

Screech. The mail dude nudges the cart, then jumps, like he's scared himself.

I scooch out of the way and the squeaky cart rolls on by.

"I didn't lie about my allergy! And what the hell do you mean you 'took a chance' on me?" I can think of *plenty* of ways to interpret that remark, and not a single one is good.

His voice feels like a sharp blade being dragged just gently enough across my throat to leave a scrape. "You lied by omission."

Declan's lips are tight and his eyes are anywhere but on me. There's nothing I can say, is there? He's decided in his own rat brain that he's done with me. All this "which Shannon are you?" crap is just that—crap. He's hiding something, and it's pretty damn obvious. To me.

I was good for a screw in the limo and the lighthouse and...well, for that, but I'm not good enough to date in front of Daddy. He's just like Steve, only the stakes, and dollar signs, are bigger.

Did I mess up? Sure. But his reaction is so utterly out of proportion with the facts.

Plus—I'm done. Done explaining myself to irrational people who seem to care only about proving they're right. If who I really am doesn't fit into his image of who I am, then he can go suck it.

"I can't make you believe me," I say with a voice that is surprisingly even. "I don't want to."

That makes him look at me. *Really* look at me. The first sign of hesitation flashes in his eyes.

"In fact, if you can't even listen to me try to explain what's happened over the past day, then we never had one iota of what you claimed we had."

His eyes soften.

"You said a lot of things to me, too, Declan. And I remember every one of them. And you know what I'm remembering most of all?"

He just stares at me.

"When we were kissing at the restaurant that first night, you said: *He has no power over you. He discarded you. Don't give him that power back. You are worth so much more.*"

Declan's turn to look like he's been slapped.

My own eyes narrow into tight bands as I take my time, letting his own words thrown back at him sink in. His jaw grinds but he says nothing, though his eyes are so conflicted.

"You know what? I *am* worth so much more. You don't want to hear me out? Too bad. Coffee offer rescinded. Deal off and over. Everything's off the table. Good day, Declan. Have a nice life."

"Shannon," he says as if making an involuntary sound. It's not a groan or a growl or even a question. Just a statement.

"I'm either authentic and real or I'm fake and cunning. I'm one or the other. You don't even get to choose anymore, Declan. You took that choice away from yourself."

I turn on my heel to leave, and then casually throw my final words over my shoulder.

"You can't have *both*."

"I don't want both. I want the real Shannon.

And since *you* don't know who that is…"

A tingling red ball of rage takes over. Steve dumped me because I wouldn't turn myself into a pretzel and *stop* being myself. Declan insists that the "real" me, whatever that is, isn't enough either. I can't win.

So I'm done playing.

"You know what, Declan?"

Silence from him. Just that cold, green resolve in eyes that used to smile on me.

"Go validate yourself." It takes everything in me not to give him the bird as I walk away.

Chapter Three

"This is the part where I'm supposed to say he's an asshole and she's so much better off without him," Amy whispers to Amanda as I go through my seventh tissue in five minutes, "but I can't honestly say that."

I am on my bed, wearing an old pair of velour pants that I think my grandma left at Mom's house before she died. My torn pink shirt—the same one I wore the day I met Declan—is technically *on* my body, but I've been wearing it for three days straight now. It could animate of its own accord and walk away. Can bacteria become sentient? If so, my shirt has become a form of artificial intelligence.

And I smell like bacon and cookie dough. Don't ask.

"Whoever said breakups are a time for honesty?" Amanda whispers back.

"But I can't even lie about Declan!" Amy insists. "The guy's really perfect."

Amanda murmurs something in agreement.

"I can hear you!" I wail. "And you're right! That's why this hurts so much!"

Amanda rushes over with the half-melted pint of ice cream. I can't even bring myself to take a bite. That's how bad this is—a breakup where I don't eat myself into oblivion.

It's the Breakupocalypse.

"Get it away from me," I mutter. Chuckles comforts me by settling in my lap and rubbing his puckered asshole up and down my arm. Nice. Not only have I not showered in two days, I can't touch ice cream, but now I smell like cat butt.

I wonder if I feed him coffee cherries if I could make cat poop coffee from it and—

Then I remember Declan is the one who told me about cat poop coffee. I can't even look at Chuckles' butt without being reminded of the biggest mistake I ever made.

I make another mistake by saying that aloud. "Chuckles' butt reminds me of Declan." I sniff.

"She's turning into our mother," Amy whispers to Amanda without moving her lips.

"So it's bad enough I lose Declan, now I'm turning into *Moooooooom*," I wail. "That's like learning your dog died and you have a bot fly larva growing on your labia."

Amanda peels my laptop out of my fingers. "Someone's been watching way too many zit-popping videos on YouTube today," she mutters.

"She's been holed up in here all weekend, logging in to work and doing reports. She says she doesn't need to step outside for anything for at least nine days because of a batch of new, overeager mystery shoppers who will do all the in-person work for her and she just has to manage paperwork," Amy tells Amanda.

"When did you get a penis?" I ask my sister.

All the eyebrows in the room except mine hit

the ceiling. "When did I what?" Amy asks.

"You mansplained that perfectly. Over-explaining something that didn't need to be over-explained, with just enough condescension to make me hate you. Perfecto!"

"She's losing it," Amanda murmurs out of one corner of her mouth.

"I already lost it. Lost him. Lost my dignity. Lost…everything." I lean forward in a slumping motion. A cloud of fleas bounces around me.

I really am ripe.

Or Chuckles is infested.

"He's a shallow asshole!" Amanda says with about as much sincerity as Mom telling me she really liked my hair when I dyed it purple in eleventh grade.

"He's not. He's so damn amazing, and I—he—we…" I snatch my laptop back from Amanda and pop it open. "I just don't know what the hell happened. None of it makes any sense. All I know is it's all Jessica Coffin's fault."

I navigate to a zit video that features a man who appears to have a white-nippled breast growing out of his love handle. A woman bearing a heated pair of tweezers and wearing purple latex gloves performs backyard surgery while a group of relatives sit around a picnic table eating ambrosia salad.

My people. These are my people. This video will be—

"AUGH! GROSS! TURN THAT CRAP OFF!" Amy screams. Chuckles gets up and sits on my keyboard, making the video fast forward with no sound. No satisfying mashed potato goo coming out of the skin of people who view pus as entertainment.

People like...*me*.

"What have I become?" I moan. "I'm one of those weirdoes who watches zit videos."

"You're a woman who doesn't understand why her asshole ex did what he did," Amy soothes.

"And a weirdo," Amanda adds.

"That was last year. That was Steve. How can this happen to me again. How? Something is wrong with me. I'm damaged somehow. Invisibly damaged. I'm doomed to never understand why men flee from me. Why I'm not good enough. What the fatal flaw inside me is that drives men away."

"It might be the lack of showers," Amanda says softly.

I throw Chuckles at her and walk away.

"That was not supportive," Amy hisses.

"I was about to shove Vicks VapoRub up my nostrils."

"So it wasn't just me?" Amy sounds relieved.

"I CAN HEAR YOU!"

"Then go shower!" they say in unison.

"A few more emails," I mutter. A batch of new mystery shopper applications has come in. I routinely process them. It's a formality, just a series of emails I have to open and read because—

"Marie Jacoby?" I shout. Does one of the emails really say my mother's name on it?

Amanda presses her lips together to hide a

smirk.

"Mom is now a registered mystery shopper with Consolidated Evalu-shop? What the hell?"

"She wanted to do the marital aid shops, and some others, so I walked her through the steps for certification." In order to get the really good mystery shopping jobs, you have to take an online certification course. It's not hard, but it's no cake walk, either.

Pay a fee and boom—certified for a year.

"Mom did all that? It's bad enough Carol does some of my shops, but MOM?"

"She said that if the company's paying for her to try out new warming gels, sign her up."

"I refuse to be her supervisor," I say flatly.

Amanda looks alarmed, and then we both find the answer. "Josh!"

"Josh is a techie," Amy says.

"He handles overflow," I explain.

"Josh is so cute."

"He's gay."

"I know!"

"So Josh can take over with Mom," I say, forwarding her info to him. There is no way in hell I am mystery shopping nipple clamps with my mother. The sad part is, she'd be better at those shops than anyone else I know.

Sad.

"Quit stalling and get in the shower." Amanda takes the laptop from me and shuts it firmly.

"I showered regularly for Declan!" I protest. "That's not why he dumped me." The steam rises from the shower head as I strip down. Amy and Amanda are in the threshold, like I'm on some sort of watch I don't know about. Are they worried I'll harm myself? The worst damage I could inflict would be eating two entire packaged of peanut-butter-stuffed Oreos, and if they think their presence will prevent that, well...

Too late.

"Jessica Coffin has some blame here," Amy says in an ominous voice. "Poking him on Twitter."

"He never cared about Twitter," I call out. The rhythm and flow of cleansing myself helps. Lather, rinse, lather, rinse, conditioner, leave it on. Soap and clean the filth off me. Rinse. It's a ritual cleansing. Normally I'd cry in the shower, but my sister and best friend are outside sharing theories about Why Declan Dumped Shannon, and while there's plenty of fodder for material, the way they're talking is such a relief.

Because they're just as perplexed as I am.

The lesbian thing? He knows I'm not. His fury at thinking I'd been using him to climb the corporate ladder and land a big client? C'mon. Couldn't he tell by how my body, my heart, my lips, and hands responded to him that I was—am—sincerely falling for him?

Is he a commitmentphobe? Am I just a fat chick he decided to bone because he could? Does he harbor the same snotty pretense that Steve has about wanting a more refined woman? Did my bee allergy turn him off? What what what?

My mind is my own worst enemy, looping

frantically through every possible scenario to understand what my heart already knows:

He's gone.

But why?

And if I can't have him back, then how can I get through the minutes that become hours, the hours that become days, and the days that roll out and on and on without sharing a look with him? A hug or a kiss, or a casual wink that holds so much promise?

Who else on the planet could I meet with my hands down a toilet and have them ask me out on a date?

(One without a toilet fetish, I mean. There are 588 people on FetLife looking for women who put their hands in toilets. That's not an imaginary number—I checked.)

I turn on the waterproof radio Amy uses when she showers. "Ain't No Sunshine" pours loud and proud through the tiny bathroom, and that?

That gives me permission to cry in the shower. Big, fat, ugly tears of pain and abandon. Of promises that just died, of hope that was murdered, of the sound of his name rushing in to fill all the cracks in my mind.

Declan.

How do you drive away the very thing you once welcomed so eagerly just weeks ago?

You start by letting it leak out through your eyes.

I hear the door close quietly and I cry under the hot water for as long as I have tears. My mouth is so dry it should have sand in it. Maybe this is how I try to block out the last few days: death by intentional dehydration via tears.

A soft knock on the door shocks me. "What? You don't barge in on me anymore? Oh, dear sweet Jesus, am I that bad off that you're walking on eggshells around me?"

"Mom called," Amy says.

"And?" I shout, turning the water off.

"She wants you to go to her yoga class tonight, after you're done with work. Says it will be good for you."

As I dry off, I groan. "All those old ladies will ask where Declan is!"

"Think of it as a Golden Girls gripefest."

"That's not helping."

"Mom will take you out for ice cream afterwards."

"Not helping either." I am sliding my underwear on over my hips and it appears they have shrunk.

"It's really bad," Amy says to Amanda.

"I can hear you through the door, you know! Those cheap hollow core pieces of crap Dad's always complaining about are about as effective at hiding your comments as Mom is at being tactful."

"Yoga. 7:15. That's the message."

"Fine!" I choke out, talking to the steam. "I'll meet her! But I'm getting toffee *allllll* over my double chocolate chip ice cream and she has to tolerate the crunching!" I shout.

"I'll text her for you so she can bring ear

plugs."

I make a sound of disgust so deep in my throat I think I've inherited a hairball from Chuckles.

"Amanda and I are leaving now," Amy declares.

"But we'll be back tomorrow!" Amanda shouts.

"Of course you will," I call back. "You have to deconstruct my failure."

"With pad Thai! My treat!" she shouts back. I hear the front door close.

Yoga class, huh?

An image of Declan's tight, muscled ass in workout clothes at the only yoga class he attended makes my heart race, my mouth feel like sandpaper, and parts farther south get moist. Moister than they are from the shower. And then the tears return.

One of the hardest parts about breaking up with someone is that moment when you realize they will never, ever touch you again. Not once. Not one stroke, one love pat, one kiss, one lick, one thrust—nothing. Dry and barren defines your new relationship, and the deep intensity, the push and pull, the dance that was all-consuming in getting to know them and defining and redefining boundaries, it's all…gone.

Just gone.

All done.

Over and out.

Forever.

I'm never going to have Declan lace his fingers through mine. *Never* rest his palm on my ass and squeeze. *Never* thread his fingers through my hair and tug gently as he kisses me with such urgency you'd think we had to make love before the house stopped burning.

Never.

Never is a long time.

Never makes me cry again.

Never is the loneliest word.

Never.

Chapter Four

When I arrive at Mom's yoga class, the room is at capacity. Packed. Sixty women and one older man are in the room. I do a double take at the man.

"Fire marshal," Mom explains. I jump and make a little sound of surprise, because she's like a vampire. So swift I didn't realize she was there.

"Fire marshal?"

"There might be too many people in the room. Someone called him in."

"What's going on? Is Sting here or something? Willem Dafoe? Alec Baldwin's wife?"

"Ha ha. Hilaria Baldwin. She's a famous yoga instructor, but nope! None of those people are the reason." Mom beams at me and looks around behind me. "Where's Declan?"

Ah. Now I get it. Hoo boy. Mom has a thousand-dollar yoga class and I get to be the bearer of bad news. What a great way to get restoration.

"He's not here."

"Running late?"

"No. Not coming. We broke up." Oh, those last words. They feel, literally, like last words. Someone should shake some holy water on me and I'll just go into Savasana and everything can slip away.

Not really. No guy is worth that.

"You broke up with a billionaire? Are you

insane? They don't grow on trees!"

The image of Declan hanging from a branch, sweet and ripe and ready to be plucked, isn't helping.

"I'm...sorry? I'm not sure what to say." Tears threaten the edges of my eyes. No no no. Can't cry in front of a group of women drooling to stare at my ex-boyfriend's butt.

"Oh, honey!" Mom's trying to be supportive at the same time that she's freaking out on the inside, because Declan was obviously her Big Draw.

"I'm not leaving!" I hear Agnes shout to the poor fire marshal, who looks a bit panicked.

"No one has to leave, ma'am," he says. The guy looks just enough like Dad to make me look again. "But I do need to ask that the class be capped at seventy people, and that the two exits remain open at all times."

"Who called him?" I cock a suspicious eyebrow at Agnes as I try to change the subject.

"Probably Agnes. I'll bet she hoped he'd clear the room and she could sneak in to get the prime spot behind Declan. She's offering an entire unlimited class card for two months if people will back off."

"Who knew a billionaire's butt was so valuable," I crack, and then...I really crack. A tight ball of sorrow fills my throat and my ears burn. The tears come now and Mom's arms are around me, one hand smoothing my hair, messing up the ponytail.

"Oh, Shannon, it's going to be okay. It will. I

don't know what to say right now," she adds, twisting her head and looking helplessly around the room.

"I know. I didn't want to tell you, but—"

"I want to know the rest. Really. I want to know the entire story, but right now…"

I wipe the tears off my face with a little yoga towel. "Gotcha." I sniff and compose myself.

And then:

"SHANNON!" Jesus, Agnes has some strong lungs for a woman who looks like a desiccated Hobbit. "Where's Declan?" The leer on her face as she says his name takes three decades off her.

"He's not here. Sorry," I peep.

Silence. All shuffling and whispers and movement halts.

"Not here. Running late?"

Good God.

"No," I say, extending the word with a tone of contrition. "He's just not coming. Sorry."

"Why are you sorry?" Corrine asks. "You're not him. You have nothing to be sorry about."

And that makes the waterworks come pouring out.

A sudden rush of women surround me, hands patting my back, wrapped around my shoulders, soothing me. Out of the corner of my eye I see a few women scowl and trickle out of the room.

The fire marshal is noticeably relieved.

Mom is in the middle of the group. Their hands and throaty sounds of comfort are so kind that I can't hold back. Grief and fear and reproach and regret pour out of me in a string of sobs so disjointed they sound like a new modern music composition.

And then the questions begin. Oh, the questions.

"Did he cheat on you? I read an article in *Science News* about how men with higher status cheat on their mates more than men with lower social status and income. So maybe you need to aim lower."

Aim lower?

Corrine jostles Agnes hard enough for the two to look like bone-thin weeble-wobbles, frantically grasping at each other to avoid falling. Two other women in the group help them to stay upright.

"That's silly," Corrine grouses. "I've known men who were gas station attendants making minimum wage who were cheaters. You don't need to be a billionaire."

"He didn't cheat on me," I say, sighing. Every attempt to catch Mom's eye is met with the careful avoidance Mom has honed with the care of a neurosurgeon removing a tumor with tendrils that spread out like the Flying Spaghetti Monster.

"Bad in bed?" Agnes asks. Every eyebrow is arched now. All breathing has paused. Enraptured, the crowd slowly closes in as if I'm about to spill the salacious details.

"Uh, no."

One big exhale. "Good. Last thing I need is to have that fantasy destroyed."

What?

"If you're going to date a hot, rich man he'd better be good in bed, too. Otherwise, the myth is as boring as sleeping with a guy who thinks taking out the garbage for you is foreplay and whose idea of cuddling is to reach over you afterward to grab the *TV Guide*."

"Ladies!" Mom claps her hands. It's the sound of rescue. "Time to get started." She looks like a blonde Michelle Bachmann teaching pre-schoolers. Crazy eyes and big smiles abound.

"Wait, Marie," Agnes shouts. She's wearing magenta lycra bike shorts and a t-shirt that says [insert funny saying]. Seriously—that's what it says. Just the brackets and "insert funny saying." I like Agnes more and more every time I see her. "We need to know more about Declan. Why did you two break up?"

Mom ignores her. "Some of you have already met her, but this is my middle daughter, Shannon. She's the one who dated a billionaire and then she pretended to be a lesbian for her job and got outed."

Oh. My. God.

The old woman next to me pats my hand. "It gets better, dear."

"Lesbians?" another old woman sniffs. "We didn't have those when I was younger."

"Oh, she's not really gay. She just acts like it when she has to do mystery shops. And when she ruins her life." Mom fluffs her hair and turns to her iPod, poking the screen. Languid music fills the air, but it's not enough to stop the lambs from screaming in my head.

37

Corrine's face lights up. "If he thinks you're a lesbian, then here's your solution: call your wife and call Declan and offer him a threesome."

Disturbing murmurs of assent fill the air. Even the fire marshal is listening now.

Especially the fire marshal.

"Every man wants two women at once," Agnes adds.

"We tried that once," Mom says. The entire crowd turns its focus to her. While it's a relief to be out from under scrutiny, having Mom talk about her and Dad getting it on with another woman is about as much fun as going to a feminist rally with Robin Thicke.

"You did?" someone asks. The fire marshal is now leaning against the wall. Pretty soon I expect to see him smoking a cigarette and talking about how this was the best capacity check he's ever had.

"We were going to go to one of those meet-up things where you find other people online who have the same, uh...tastes." Mom makes actual eye contact with me for a second and it appears—sweet Jesus!—even she has an oversharing limit.

"What happened?" I ask, turning the tables.

"Jason chickened out." *Not you?* I want to ask.

"Not you?" Agnes asks. If I were standing closer to her I'd give her a fist bump.

"I...well, anyhow," she says, weirdly avoiding the question. "We just bought one of those 'real dolls' and had at it."

The entire room is struck dumb.

"You had sex with a doll?" Agnes finally asks.

38

"This alone is worth the $17 fee," Corrine whispers to a group of shocked women.

"*I* didn't have sex with it. But…"

"Dad did?" I squeak. Brain bleach. Brain bleach. You cannot un-hear that.

She claps her hands twice. "Topic change! Let's start out in Child's Pose."

"You can't just cut us off in the middle of something that salacious! How many of us here have had husbands who humped a woman-shaped version of water wings?" Corrine shouts.

Three women raise their hands.

Kink is the new black.

"This is supposed to be restorative yoga!" I hiss to the group, eyes blazing and on Mom. "I did not come here under duress to listen to people talk about their partners humping plastic sex dolls."

"Well, dear," Agnes huffs, "we didn't come here to listen to you tell us how you destroyed a fantastic relationship with a billionaire with an ass so fine you could hang it on a wall at the Museum of Fine Arts."

More murmurs of assent.

"So no one is getting what they want today!" Mom says in a too-cheerful voice. "Let's forget about kinky sex and settle in to taking a nice, meditative breathing session."

Groans of dissent.

As we crawl on our mats, Agnes leans over and says in a scratchy voice, "Make sure the next boyfriend is eye candy, too, and I'll buy you a new pair of yoga pants.'

"The poor woman lost Boston's hottest eligible bachelor, Agnes. We should buy her a consolation prize."

"A vibrator that smells like money?"

That was Corrine. I just...I can't sit here and talk about sex toys with a woman who looks like my second grade teacher. Can't.

Won't.

"And now we relax," Mom intones as deep chimes tones fills the air.

Yeah.

Right.

Chapter Five

"You *did* lose a billionaire," Mom says as she joins me, sitting at the booth at the local ice cream parlor, my spoon digging into a puddle of caramel and marshmallow sauce that is about as viscous as any salacious fluid I've ever put in my mouth before (and considerably tastier). "It takes a certain kind of skill to drive a man like that away."

"I love you, too, Mom," I mumble after shoving the chocolate-chip-caramel-marshmallow love in my mouth. That's right—love. I can buy a giant glass full of sugared love. The proof fills my tongue with a sweet coating of love, the cold chocolate bliss biting into my teeth and gums, my stomach groaning with anticipatory pleasure as my six dollars buys me a gustatory hug, kiss, and if you add in the peanut butter sauce in the ramekin on the side—maybe even an ass grab.

"I don't mean to rub salt in the wound, honey."

"Then why are you standing there with a brick of Himalayan salt the size of my head and beating me with it?"

She purses her lips in what looks like a Chuckles' butt imitation, then softens. "I'm sorry. You're right."

I freeze, and not from an ice cream headache. I go completely still.

"Say what?" I choke out.

Mom rolls her eyes. "I can admit when I'm wrong." Her own glass full of love is perched in front of her, a bunch of berry-flavored nonsense covered in more berries, with whipped cream on top. This is how I know we cannot possibly be related, because my mother only eats berry-flavored ice cream. No chocolate sauce, no caramel-y gooey joy. She won't touch cookie dough ice cream, nor butter pecan, nor anything with chunks of chocolate in it.

That's just…it's like she's a poor imitation of someone who possesses XX chromosomes. Like she's a Stepford Wife. The only thing worse would be to hate ice cream, and if I ever meet someone who does I'll have to pull out the microchip embedded in their neck and scream, "POD PERSON!"

I just stare at her. I feel so hollow. I'm so empty the ice cream on my spoon starts to drip back in the sundae glass.

Her lips snap shut and she gives me a look of compassion so deep and authentic it makes tears well in my eyes.

"You're really hurting, honey."

All I can do is nod.

"I wish I could make it better."

"You said the same thing when Steve dumped me, Mom."

"I meant it then, too." She's a little disheveled after yoga, a little less done today, makeup lighter, her hair perfectly in place and hairsprayed so well it would take a Category 4 hurricane to blow a single strand out of place, but she's more…Mom. More of the woman who tucked me in bed with a nighttime story, the mother who catered to me when I was sick, the one who taught me how to use an EpiPen by injecting herself in the thigh seventeen times before I got it right.

The mom who just is *there*. A steady presence. We joke and she needles (pun intended) and is overbearing and judgmental, but she's Mom no matter what. She'll love me no matter what. She will invade my apartment and respect boundaries about as well as Vladimir Putin and chime a wine glass to get me to kiss a billionaire client and over-babble about her sex life with Dad, but by God, she's got my back.

And right now I need her more desperately than I need a shower.

And that is saying *a lot*.

Using her Mommy Sense, which is like Spidey Sense but with more judgment, she stands, walks to my side of the booth, moves closer to me, and just opens her arms. A whiff of something floral and spicy fills the air between us and then I'm in her warm embrace, crying so hard I will probably leave a salt lick on her shoulder, and I get to fade away for a few precious minutes and stop being Shannon, stop being the stupid woman who blew it with the best guy ever, stop being the feminist career woman who can't believe Declan is such an ass, and—

I can just cry and be held by my mommy.

Who is murmuring something unintelligible in

43

my ear, but it sounds like she's saying, "Like father, like son."

"Huh?" I pull back. The steel blue of her lightweight rayon jacket has a brow-shaped wet spot on it.

"Like father, like son," she says, a scowl making her crow's feet emerge.

"What do you mean?"

"James." She says his name like it's a curse word.

"What about James?"

Silence. Mom doesn't do silence. The hair on my arms starts to stand on end.

"Mom?"

She shifts uncomfortably in her seat, spooning the perfect ratio of whipped cream, berry ice cream, and fresh berries onto a spoon. Then she stuffs the entire concoction in her mouth so she can't talk.

"When you swallow, the truth is coming out."

"That's what *he* said," are the first words out of her mouth.

"What does that even mean?"

"I was making a joke. You know. He. Swallow. Um…"

"Joke fail."

Her eyes narrow. "It's never, *ever* not funny to joke about swallowing."

I regard my marshmallow cream in a whole new light and drop my spoon. "Thanks, Mom. You just ruined my chocolate comfort."

"It's not like you need the sugar."

"Since when do you criticize my eating habits?

44

That's like Paula Deen telling Dr. Oz how to eat."

She frowns. "Let's talk about Declan."

"Let's not. Let's talk about James. His dad. Who you...know?"

She turns the same shade of pink as her ice cream. "I don't know how to talk about him."

My mind races to do the math. "You can't possibly know him from anywhere. He's at least ten years older than you."

"Seven."

My turn to narrow my eyes. I feel like a snake, ready to hiss, or hug her to death. "Spill it."

She bats her eyelashes innocently. "Spill what?"

"Two seconds ago you were doing heavy-duty mother-daughter bonding over what an ass Declan and his father are—"

"Not Declan. Just his father."

"Spill it!" I shout, slamming my fist on the tabletop. She flinches.

Anger feels so much better than depression.

"We dated."

My turn to flinch.

"Oh, God. We're both sampling from the same male gene pool?"

She frowns. "This is a bad time to make a swallow joke, isn't it?"

I shove my ice cream away and start to gag. Maybe another hairball from Chuckles.

Mom primly wipes her mouth and sighs, leaning forward conspiratorially. "I dated James very briefly when I was young and single and working in Boston as a stripper."

"WHAT? When were you a stripper? Does Dad know?" I knew Mom worked as an artist's assistant years ago and had memorized her stories about living in abandoned warehouses in the scummier parts of the city, but this?

"That's right," she says calmly. "When I stripped the canvases for the—"

"A paint stripper," I say, relieved.

She looks confused. "What did you think I meant—oh, dear!" Her laughter sounds like bells tinkling. "You thought I meant I took off my clothes for money?"

"That's the generally accepted definition of 'stripper,' Mom."

"When I take my clothes off for a man, I don't expect to get paid for it."

I just blink.

"Okay, maybe dinner and a movie..."

"You're just prolonging the inevitable here, Mom. You dated my boyfriend's father?"

"Ex-boyfriend. Ex-boyfriend, dear."

"You rang?" says a familiar voice.

No. Not Declan. This story would be so much better if it were, but...

It's Steve.

Chapter Six

"You have the most interesting conversations, Marie," Steve says with an unctuous tone so slick you could dip focaccia bread in it.

"And you have the uncanny ability to appear in the most unusual places," I mumble.

"Like a fairy godfather," he says with a disarmingly sweet smile.

"Like a psycho stalker," I retort. My mouth goes dry. I can't stop looking at his eyes. He seems almost...appealing. But that voice. It's like he's being warm and sweet at the same time he's convincing me to invest in a Bernie Madoff scheme.

"I like my answer better," he challenges, the sweetness gone suddenly. I sigh with relief, because the dissonance was too hard.

"That's because you're a bit unhinged," I say. Loudly, as I reach for my sundae and shove more chocolate goo in my mouth. "Go away, Steve."

He cackles. It sounds like Dr. Evil, high on NyQuil. "*I'm* the unhinged one? You pretend to be a lesbian and double-cross your billionaire ex and *I'm* unhinged?"

"Double-cross?" Mom asks, curling her arm around her ice cream protectively. "Shannon double-crossed someone?"

He pauses and stands awkwardly. If Mom asks

him to join us, all bets are off.

"She cozied up to Declan McCormick and slept with him to get some big accounts for her company. All while pretending to be a lesbian," he declares. He's wearing a simple white button-down shirt, khakis, and Crocs. Steve is the only man I know who insists that Crocs count as business casual wear. Sure. For nurses.

"How do you know she was pretending?" Mom asks. The catch in her voice makes the tops of my ears go hot. She's up to something. I wish Chuckles were here, because I could read his frowns to understand better what Mom's ulterior motive is. I'm on my own, though. No Kitty Radar in an ice cream shop.

"Because I dated her for two years and I would know if I had slept with a lesbian," he replies, voice dripping with sarcasm thicker than the impenetrable layer of ego that he wraps himself in, like a forcefield of arrogance everyone else knows is invisible, but he thinks is Kevlar.

"How would you know if you slept with a lesbian?" Mom asks again. "Is a lesbian's vagina a different texture? Do they use a code word during sex? Do they bring a U-Haul on the first date? Do they refuse to perform blow jobs on you?"

Steve's jaw drops a little and he starts breathing through his mouth.

I keep mine shut and sit back, ready to watch Mom in all her glory. It's kind of nice to watch her turn this on someone other than me.

"Uh, I, uh…" he says.

She turns to me with a pseudo-accusatory look on her face. "Shannon, is that why Steve was always so uptight? You wouldn't play the flesh flute?"

Marshmallow cream comes flying out my nostrils as I choke to death. It's a hell of a way to go. I imagine the Stay Puft Marshmallow Man greets you in heaven on a white cloud of fluff.

She points at me and grasps Steve's arm. "See? She can do it with ice cream. I'd imagine that marshmallow cream tastes better than—"

"Mom!" I cough. I'm not rescuing Steve. I'm preserving my nasal passages, because if she makes another comment about fellatio I'm going to shoot hot fudge so far into my sinus cavity I'll have yeast infections in my brain.

"My sex life is none of your business," Steve says in a cold voice.

"I did," I tell Mom, pretending Steve's not here. "But let's just say it wasn't an even trade."

Steve's eyes fly so far open his irises look like they're swimming in a bowl of cream. Marshmallow cream.

"You can't talk about blow jobs with your mother! That's…private," he insists.

"Like feeding Jessica Coffin stories to tweet is private?" I say sweetly.

"So you went up the elevator but you wouldn't go down," Mom needles Steve.

"I…what? No, it's not…I didn't…you don't…" *Give up*, I want to tell him. You're just digging the hole deeper, and that's just more rope

Mom needs to get to lower the bucket of lotion to you.

She turns to me and pats my hand. "Poor thing. No wonder you didn't fight him when he dumped you. It was a blessing. Being with a selfish, egotistical blowhard is one thing. But a selfish, egotistical blowhard who is bad in bed isn't ever worth it."

Steve looks like someone just removed his voice box with a corkscrew. His mouth opens and closes, his eyes jumping like little fleas trying to find a safe place to land. He's struggling to think and speak and react and I get the distinct impression that this conversation is not going as planned.

"I did not say a word to Jessica," he argues, eyes shrinking to tiny, piggish triangles. Ah—so he's going to address that and ignore the giant sucking chest wound that Mom just gave him over his, well...giant suckage as a sex partner.

He's hovering over us, shifting his weight from one hip to the other, and leaning down. A veritable tower of terror, I tell you. I am afraid for his dignity, which is about as likely to remain intact as a rock star's t-shirt in a mosh pit.

"*Someone* fed her the story," I retort.

"I'm not that someone."

"Then it was Monica."

He snorts. It makes him sound like a manatee. "My mother and Jessica aren't close."

"Monica isn't capable of being close to anyone," Mom says. "It would ruin her varnish."

Steve frowns. "That's my mother you're

insulting."

"Yes," Mom says. "It is."

"Why did I even come over here?" he asks the air, waving his hands around as if he has an audience. Every single person in the store ignores him, because in the battle for attention between Steve and a giant peanut butter fudge sundae, he's losing. Big time.

"We were wondering the same thing," Mom and I say in unison.

"Maybe to apologize for being so selfish in bed with Shannon?" Mom adds in a voice that carries through the ice cream parlor at the exact moment the satellite radio station pauses between songs. Now Steve's got all the attention he wants. And he clearly doesn't want it.

"Dude," says a college student, a guy sleeved with tattoos. "That's sad," he says as he walks out carrying a loaded ice cream cone the size of my cat's head.

"Would you please tell your mother," Steve hisses, bending down to whisper in my ear, "that I was not...that I...that she's..."

This is the part where, for two long years, I anticipated what he wanted me to say and played puppy dog to whatever he wanted. I used to wag my tail and eagerly jump up and do what he wanted, including fetching the same stick 127 times in a row.

I got accustomed to being in a state of panic when my man was being challenged by someone else, especially when he was a douchebag who would take it out on me emotionally, later, when all the people who had a deep core that was strong enough to call him on his bull were gone. Conditioned to becoming the peacemaker, the neutralizer, she-who-must-appease-the-overinflated-ego-in-a-skinbag, I felt the cold flush of fear that he was going to overreact.

But that was then. And *then* is long gone.

I let my heart beat once. Twice, Three times. Ten. The silence between beats is excruciating. It feels like an eternity, with Mom watching Steve with shrewd eyes that are zeroed in on him now that he's maimed, and she's waiting for him to bleed out enough to go in for the kill.

And then another space between beats. Another. One more, all with Steve giving me that *look*. The one that holds expectations—thousands of them, carefully cultivated over years together, his well-worn reflex of knowing I'll jump right in and —what?

Save him?

Silence. Heartbeats. Spaces between.

I need to save *me*.

I look him in the eye and say the exact same words he used on me, more than a year ago, when he broke up with me.

"I'm sorry, Steve. It's just that you were never really up to par for what I need."

One corner of Mom's mouth tips up and her fingers twitch. She wants to high-five me, and the muscles in her neck tighten. She wants to say something but breathes through her nose instead, captivated but uncharacteristically quiet.

Steve has this expression of patience that melts into disbelief, as if his brain is on a three-second delay. He's finally realizing that I'm not going to rescue him. Coddle him. Prop up the mythology that says he's the center of the universe, that his emotional core is radioactive and therefore must be protected from exposure at all costs. He's trained me to believe that it's my responsibility to buy into his idea that he's above criticism, and anyone who dares to confront him is ignorant and worthy only of derision.

Silence and non-movement are my weapons now. And while I'm clumsy and unskilled, I'm using them to protect my core.

Finally.

This is what Declan meant about Steve. Not letting him make me feel inferior. Except Declan was wrong.

Dead wrong.

It wasn't that I let Steve make me feel lesser.

It was that I let him convince me that the order of the world demanded that I *am* lesser.

And I'm seeing now that the way the world works isn't some pre-defined set of rules that other people get to make and impose on me.

Steve finds his voice. "I'm done." And he just walks away with fisted hands and a tight jaw.

"So am I," I say in a clear, but calm voice, pushing the ice cream away.

Mom's speechless.

Which means I won in so many more ways.

Chapter Seven

The slide of his hands, soft palms with squared fingernails moving out of my vision as he cradles my face, makes me inhale slowly, devouring the taste of his breath. We're in bed, nude, skin against skin and heat against heat, the combination turning us into a fireball of sensual desire.

Desire that will soon convert and combust into a licking flame.

I've waited so long for this, the press of his fingertips into my belly, the slow crawl of his mouth over my breast, the warm wetness of his mouth, his tongue tracing circles that make me taut with a craving for his taste. My body is a landscape for him to explore and I sink my hands into Declan's hair, the long strands a surprise. He's growing it out, a stark contrast to his short, clipped look, and when he catches my eye with a jaunty grin, one half-curl pops over his eyebrow and makes me fall in love all over again.

Again.

As if there could be more.

The space between us is so small you can't fit a heart in there, much less two. We'll have to share one that beats enough for us both as his mouth finds mine and says, "I'm here." The next kiss says that he's here to stay, and then that turns out to be a tiny white lie as he travels the valley to the sweet, supple parts of me that are so achingly ready for his mouth, his fingers, his throbbing flesh, our pounding need.

He's back, in my bed, and it's like he never left. Bright green eyes with tiny flecks of brown and topaz at the edge of the pupils are so close that I can read the colors. If I had the gift of second sight I could tell you what his orbs tell the world about all the dimensions of love we share, but I'm woefully incapacitated as he captures my red nub, enticing and teasing, mouth exploring where I tremor with anticipation.

"Beautiful," he murmurs in a voice I know so well, using words I've heard before, in the limo, on a lighthouse floor, in my own bed.

My own bed, where I am right now.

With him.

"I've missed you. Missed—" My breath hitches, the words broken in half as he splits me with an expert touch that does exactly what he wants, that draws all the blood from my inner self to the surface, giving him a wonderful playland to use as he pleases, for pleasure and joy.

"Missed me?" Declan pulls up, then murmurs in my ear, tongue loose and leisurely on my neck, the gentle kisses he peppers down the side turning into fiercer love bites. I'll have marks in the morning, little notes that play the melody of these minutes, hours in bed together.

A relief map of sorts. A cartographer's plot, charting the way to join me in ecstasy.

And yet…a chart for one and only one man to

follow.

Ever.

"You never need to miss me again, Shannon. Never." His kiss makes me clench, the friction of belly against abs like he's already in me, touching deep and unleashing a release so strong I can't hold back.

"I love you so much, Declan," I whisper.

My own hands become greedy, needing to accumulate more memory of his hot skin, wanting to memorize the contours of his marbled back, his muscled thighs, the soft skin where leg becomes sex. In the inner curve of his hip I find a place only I can excite, one that he reserves for me—and *only* me—and his next word echoes my own thoughts.

"Mine. You're mine, Shannon. Forever. Don't ever doubt me, please. Trust me. Give over to me. Let me love you. Let me show you how much I love you."

Declan's eyes have gone dark green with desire, the color of emerald velvet, like a cape spread out on a mossy hill in Ireland for two lovers to enjoy an afternoon frolic in the sun, the coast and the rush of the ocean surrounding us. He's all sea air and crash and rolling hills, dotted with the sunshine of homecoming and love everlasting.

In a flash, I'm on my back and he's over me, poised to claim me, my legs opening of their own will, my body so primed. So ready. So—

Beep beep beep.

My heart pounding, my hands fisting the sheets, and a puddle under me the size of Lake

Chargoggagoggmanchauggagoggchaubunagungama ugg (yes, it's a real lake in Massachusetts), I wake up mid-climax, thrashing a bit and shaking myself out of what is, disappointingly, just a dream.

Another damn dream.

Third one in three days.

All my pink bits are hot and wet, all my other bits are cold and tingly, and my brain bits are embarrassed as hell that I can have the female equivalent of wet dreams against my will by thinking about a man who will never touch me again.

Never.

There's that word again.

I am covered in a sheen of sweat, and oh, if only you could sweat disappointment and unrequited love out of your pores. I'd live in a sauna for a month if it could exorcise the demon of heartbreak that lives inside me, teasing me with subconscious fantasies of reunion, of unconscious motives that make me google Declan, follow him on Twitter, wish for one brush with him so we can talk it out and reunite.

I'd take a drug to make the pain go away. So far, copious amounts of chocolate have done nothing but make the pudge around my waist a little softer. If only I could drive the pain out with a master cleanse. Someone should make a protein shake and market it.

The Breakup Smoothie.

Declan's taste is in my mouth. The touch of his lips is between my breasts, so real I reach up my shirt to chase his fingers. The lingering sense that he really was here, that he really did travel across my skin and give himself to me in my curves and hollows, makes me feel haunted.

Haunted.

As the cool morning air fills in the space between dream and reality, it chases all the vestiges of my Dream Declan away, leaving me bereft.

Chilled.

Unmoored.

I grab my phone and shut off the alarm, then check my calendar. I have a mystery shop today, one in person about two hours away.

Two hours? That's a rare one. Why would I—

Oh.

Yeah.

That one.

The sex toy shop. We're being paid travel time plus our mileage to handle a series of sex toy shops, to make sure they're not selling pornographic materials to minors. And if they have a tobacco license, we're checking on cigarette sales to minors, too.

As my lady parts stop their Gangnam Style dance imitation and I catch my breath, I remember the worst part:

Mom is my partner on these.

Thoughts of Mom and a naked Declan doing unmentionably delightful things to me do not mix. It's like Baileys Irish Cream and sloe gin: warning! Warning, Will Robinson!

You throw up when you combine the two.

Chuckles climbs on my bed, sniffs my crotch, and gives me a mildly disgusted look. It's not rivetingly disgusted, though, which is alarming.

That means he's come to expect to be disappointed in me.

Or I need a shower.

Either way, even my cat thinks that my dreams are deviant.

And you can't sink much lower than that.

Or so I thought.

* * *

"I thought Amanda was doing this shop with me. Not you!" Mom grouses as we pull into the parking garage in downtown Northampton. I love the rare mystery shop that brings me into this college town, where the coffee shops are fabulous, you can find the best smoothies anywhere, and street buskers are as conversant about American foreign policy as they are about the best pad Thai in town.

But I don't relish the idea of comparison shopping vibrators with my mother. That's up there with looking forward to getting a pap smear, a root canal, and a colonoscopy at the same time.

Which I'd prefer over this.

"Me too, but she tricked me." *Tricked* is a tiny confabulation. Okay, a huge one. She offered to spend a few hours snooping on my behalf and getting some dirt on Declan if I took Mom on this sex toy mystery shop.

No bleeping way.

"Fine, then," Amanda had said. "If you don't take the sex toy shop with Marie, I'll tell her you the truth about that taping of Rachael Ray."

"You wouldn't!"

"Try me."

My mother is the biggest Rachael Ray fan EVER. I had a chance to go for a customer service evaluation last year, and Mom had begged, pleaded, and cajoled, but I'd stood firm. Being embarrassed is one thing, but on television?

I have to draw a line somewhere.

And that line brought me here to Northampton to a nearby sex toy store with my mother.

Being humiliated on the Rachael Ray show suddenly looks so much more appealing. Amanda stood her ground, and here I am...

"I can't believe they put a sex toy shop here," Mom says as we get out of the car.

"Here?" I look around at the quaint brick buildings, eyes catching the glint of sunlight off the large display window for an art gallery. "Oh, no. Not here. We're just in the parking lot to grab a good cup of coffee."

She rolls her eyes but smiles and links her arm through mine as we walk across the bridge from the car park to the shopping mall building. "You and your coffee. Why not just stop and get an iced coffee from—"

I stop her before she names a ubiquitous coffee and donut shop. I also shudder. "That's what you drink when you have no choice."

"No, Shannon—that's what you drink when you mystery shop for a living."

Twenty minutes later, *good* lattes secured, we pull out of the lot and head toward Smith College along Route 9, a slightly scenic route to our destination. I'm driving slowly, as traffic is thicker than usual, when the long, slim, swanlike body of a tall blonde catches the corner of my eye. I slow the Turdmobile down, and a guy hauling trash on a bike —a trailer full of actual garbage cans, five or so in a straight line—makes his way past me with effort.

"Nice piece of crap," he calls out in a jocular tone. Mom waves and says something friendly.

My eyes are locked on Jessica Coffin. "Yep. She sure is," I say.

A group of pedestrians clogs a zebra-striped crosswalk and I'm forced to stop, my eyes eating up the scene. It's definitely her. Without a doubt. She looks over and her eyes fix on a spot above my head, her nose wrinkling in distaste. She's seen the coffee bean on the hood of my car and correctly determined it looks more like a piece of—

Her.

My impulse to give her the finger remains firmly suppressed, though what's the harm? She can't possibly realize it's me, right?

"What are you staring at?" Mom asks.

"Jessica Coffin."

"JESSICA COFFIN?" Mom screams. And by "scream," I mean bellows like a foghorn being amplified by a Gillette Stadium sound system.

Blonde hair down in a white curtain around hips slimmer than my thigh, she shimmers as she turns and her eyes narrow. Eyes on me (or my car, or maybe my mother, who is wildly waving her arms and screaming, "Jessica! I love your tweets!"), Jessica slips her hand through the kinked elbow of a man standing with his back to the road. She leans in to his ear, whispers something, and then clings to him like a lover with casual access to her man.

In profile, the two look like something out of a *Vogue* article. A giant banner across the courtyard between the buildings announces the opening of some new children's wing near an art museum. Or a botanical garden.

The man turns just enough for me to see that it's Declan McCormick.

Maybe that new children's wing is in hell.

Cars behind me honk as I sit here, frozen, going out of my mind. Jessica and—

"DECLAN!" Mom squeals. "SO GOOD TO SEE YOU!" She's half out the window, and if I push the button and slowly close it on her, maybe she'll snap in half, ass remaining in the car with me and screaming head rolling down the street, scooped up by the next bicyclist carrying away the trash.

Speaking of trash, I look at Jessica once more, and a white wall of rage takes over my vision.

BEEP.

Mom pulls her body back in the car as someone behind me screams profanities about my feces-topped car. I hit the gas and thud into something, just hard enough for me to realize I've made a terrible error in the heat of furious passion.

A barrel of garbage goes flying up in the air and lands on the top of my car, rolls down, spewing food waste of every kind imaginable, then chunks of used tampons, and finally a thick batch of slime-coated paper.

And Mom's window is open. Wide open.

By some miracle of divine intervention (for Mom) or craptastic luck (for me), the open end of the trash can is on my side. I get an armful of what smells like composted marijuana mixed into about four cups of semen. Fermented semen, that is.

Sprouted, fair-trade, organic, non-soy spooge.

Or maybe it's just vanilla pudding. I should be reasonable here.

Jessica's derisive laugh can be heard over the screaming banshees in my head, and a thousand cars all start honking at me in unison. The people-powered garbage dude is apologizing profusely. It turns out the trash can popped out of his cart just as I hit the accelerator and it's actually not my fault.

Finally. Something's not my fault.

I fling my arm repeatedly in varying rotations of horror in an attempt to get the worst of whateverthehell that stuff is on my skin, while Declan gives me a pitying look that makes the white wall of rage come back. If small children didn't dot the crowd around Jessica and Declan I'd ram the car into them, pinning her in place and shoving the garbage can on that perfect curtain of hair while doing some revenge-type thing of undetermined specificity to Declan.

"Shannon?" Mom gasps. "Shannon, honey, you're saying the F-word over and over again and I think we need to get going."

BEEP times a thousand plus composted garbage delivered by guys who only eat paleo diets and who think mashed dates in coconut milk are "dessert" is a kind of math problem that makes me shut down. Completely.

Ignoring the mess, ignoring the honks, and flipping off the car behind me and—did she really? —Jessica and Declan, Mom storms out of her side of the car, pulls me out of the driver's seat, throws a towel she found in the back seat over the driver's side, plunks herself down, and waits for me to move all zombie-like into the passenger's side.

I'm covered in just enough slime to feel like Carrie, on stage at her prom. There's a thought. My fingers on the door handle, I stop, the sound of ten thousand horns like Buddhist gongs being struck in unison. Eyes on the building next to Jessica, I will it to crumble and crush her to death. Or a manhole cover to split her in half. An intake vent to suck in her hair and scalp her.

Thirty seconds of trying and all I get is a cloud of fruit flies in my eye. And when I go to wipe it, I get ganja-scented goo up my nose.

"Get in the car, Shannon! We have sex toys to visit!"

I am so done.

Chapter Eight

Pad Thai brought over to your bedroom by your best friend after a long day of listening to mystery shoppers give excuse after excuse for late field reports is the nectar of the gods.

Amanda shoves a piece of chicken satay in her mouth and mumbles around the meat. "That's it? He's seriously just…done? He dumped you because you pretended to be a lesbian?" We're reviewing the past week's events because we're all still in WTF mode over how my relationship fell apart.

"No, he dumped me because he thinks I dated him just to get business deals." Like that's so much better.

"And because you swing the wrong way." Amy declares this around a piece of shrimp so big it could choke her.

"I don't swing the wrong way!"

"There was that girl in college…" Amanda adds, making Amy's eyes go wide, either from shock or maybe she really is choking.

"One kiss! Everyone experiments at least once." I told Amanda that story in confidence.

Amanda and Amy shake their heads no.

"Seriously?" Now I have to add *this* to my ever-growing list of Shannon faux pas?

"I thought you were a little too good at the

credit union," Amanda says with an arched tone.

"C'mon…well, anyhow, I'm not gay and Declan knows I'm not gay. He's not upset about it. That's a red herring. Mom keeps thinking it's why he broke up with me and she's wrong."

"Then…why does he think you were only with him for the accounts?"

I retell his version of why he thinks that. By the time I'm done, Amy looks horror-stricken and Amanda is patiently picking lint balls off her cotton socks.

"Oh," they say in unison.

"Ouch," Amanda adds.

"Yep." What else can I say? Other than confessing my need to throw myself into a bottomless pit and enjoy the ride forever while thoughts of Declan torment me, there isn't much more I can explain.

"And then you saw him with Jessica Coffin at Smith College. Touching," Amy says.

Amanda waves a piece of chicken in the air and says, "But we figured that out. They're both part of that charity. Her father and his father donated more than a year's tuition at Smith to the project, so they're just there."

"Together," I groan.

"But not *together* together," Amanda insists.

"They watched me run into a garbage can and cover myself with slime."

"There are worse things," Amy says.

"Like what?"

"Being caught with your hand in a toilet in the

men's room?"

I hit her. Hard. With a piece of shrimp.

"That can't be all there is," Amy insists. She's in her running clothes, tight knee-length Lycra pants and a tank top with a built-in shelf bra, two other sports bras underneath. The Jacoby girls aren't just well endowed. We have so much breast tissue that if left unleashed, one good sudden turn to the right and we could knock out a small village.

She stretches. I reach for my ice cream. Both involve moving muscles, right? So I'm exercising right now, too. Hand, wrist, tongue, taste buds, sorrow-filled heart…

"So the whole Twitter thing happens," Amanda says in a contemplative voice. "Declan claims that he understands the lesbian thing was for work. But he says you told him in the lighthouse that you were only dating him for the account—"

"That was a *joke*!"

Amy holds up one hand to get me to pause. Amanda is deep in thought, eyes on the windowsill, staring so intently at a small basil plant that it might spontaneously turn into pesto sauce.

"—and he quoted Jessica, and then something about Steve's mother?"

Ouch. "What I said to Monica about only dating Declan for money got back to him."

"*I* said that!" Amanda protests.

"I confirmed it." A sick wave of horror pours through me. Even at the time, when I said it, I had a premonition it was a bad idea.

Now I know it. And I can't let it go. Over and

69

over, the memories of everything I ever said to Declan that might make him think I was manipulative and not earnest in my intimate moments makes me cry.

I couldn't just own up to the truth and blow the mystery shop, could I? Most people would. Instead, I tap-danced to please all the different people I thought I needed to please.

And in the end I lost the one I wanted to please the most.

"Still doesn't make sense," Amanda says, brooding. "He's not *that* shallow."

"He's *that* accustomed to being used by women for his money and connections, though," I wail. "He told me I was special because I wasn't trying to use him." The memory of his vulnerability during that conversation makes me feel like I'm two inches tall and covered in excrement. He thinks I violated that. Violated his trust.

That is what hurts the most.

Amanda's still shaking her head slowly. "I still don't buy it. You guys weren't together for that long —"

"A month." I wish it could have been forever.

"—but he's an eminently reasonable guy. You're a reasonable woman. He should have heard you out. Should have listened."

"He's overreacting," Amy concurs. "And he was kind of weird at Easter. Uptight and shy. Mom said the butter lamb freaked him out. Maybe he has a dairy phobia?"

I snorted. "No. It reminded him of his mother."

"Hmmm," Amanda says, stroking chin hairs she doesn't have. "Perhaps that's part of this."

"Huh?"

"Nothing. Let me think this through."

I'm kind of done with this conversation and now am absent-mindedly reading work email. It's the kind of day where I can get away with working from home. I don't have any mystery shops today. Just 115 emails from the people I manage.

As I open emails and scan quickly, I see we have three new approved mystery shoppers. Amanda and Amy take over the Declan analysis, trying to understand his motives, while I check out. I've worried and wondered and analyzed this issue to death, and can only come to one conclusion:

When you date a billionaire and something goes wrong, it's always your fault.

The next twenty minutes go by in a blur as I sit on the couch and process email, Chuckles eats a ficus leaf and then hairballs it up, and Amy and Amanda ignore us while strategizing.

"Earth to Shannon!" Amanda says.

"What?"

"How did Declan's mom die?"

I halt. "I...I don't know. I asked him twice and he never answered."

All six eyebrows in the room shoot up. Eight, if cats have eyebrows.

Amanda snatches the computer from me and types furiously.

And then she gasps in shock.

"Oh, Shannon. Oh my God."

71

"What?"

"Read."

The obituary Amanda pulled up on the computer screen has a breathtakingly lovely older woman's photo front and center, a thick chain of pearls around her neck, her hair pulled back in a smooth updo. Lively, friendly green eyes so familiar my heart tugs at me stare back.

Elena Montgomery McCormick.

Declan's mother.

Born in 1956. Died in 2004. She had him when she was older, and that makes James in his late fifties, which makes sense. My eyes race over the words to get them all in, and then I come to a dead stop.

Stung by the words in front of me.

The obituary is tasteful, mentioning her three kids—Terrance, Declan and Andrew—and her loving husband, James.

It's the link under it, though, that makes me hold my breath. Makes time stand still. Makes the air go thick.

The headline for a *Boston Globe* story reads:

Local business leader's wife dead from wasp sting.

Oh my God.

Amanda's hands are gentle on my shoulder as my eyes race across the page. "I can't find more about it, yet," she explains. "There isn't a major news story to explain how it happened."

"His brother had a bad incident around the same time," I tell her, brain reeling. Declan's mother died from a sting? *Died?*

"I guess this explains why he knew exactly what to do with you," Amy whispers, eyes glistening. My own throat goes salty and tight as tears I didn't know I had in me spring to the surface. The memory of that picnic, how Declan was so calm and steady yet swift and immediate, reacting with perfectly orchestrated steps, how he ran with me in his arms so far, so hard, so fast...

He saved my life and then he broke my heart.

"This can't be real," I choke out, but deep down I understand more. Suddenly. Like a clap of thunder and lightning that makes the landscape bright in a flash, revealing parts unknown, the sound echoing in a ripple of cacophony, *now* I get it.

I get it.

"He can't date me because I remind him of his mother," I say.

Amy raises one skeptical eyebrow. "You look nothing like her. For one, she has cheekbones more prominent than Heidi Klum's."

I wave my hand in the air between us. "No, not that I look like her. The sting. She had an anaphylactic allergy, I have an anaphylactic allergy. Declan can't handle it. Maybe I'm a trigger?"

Amanda makes a noise that tells me she's not convinced. "He would have dumped you right after the ER incident, then."

"It's a miracle he didn't," Amy adds with a snort. "You nearly decapitated his second head."

I give her a look that shuts her up. "Maybe he was just being nice. Not breaking up with me when

I was in a medical crisis."

"That doesn't explain Easter," she declares.

We sit in brooding silence. Amanda takes action and starts googling furiously. I take action by searching through all the open mystery shops available at work to see if there's one at a bakery. I have a hankering for muffins suddenly.

"What are you doing?" Amy asks, peering over my shoulder.

"Discovering my ex-boyfriend's mother died from the same allergy I have always makes me crave baked goods, you know?"

Amanda ignores us both. "You two leave me alone for an hour and I'll have an answer."

"What the hell am I supposed to do for an hour while I wait to find out the one little piece of information that could put all the puzzle pieces together?" I demand.

"Eat ice cream," she says.

"Okay." Good answer.

"How about we go for a nice power walk?" says my sister, Richard Simmons. In about fifty years she'll look just enough like him with that curly reddish hair…

"Power walk or ice cream. Power walk or ice cream. That's like asking if you want to have sex with Sam Heughan or just use your vibrator, Amy."

She blushes. "Some vibrators are pretty damn nice."

"Like the one I got at the sex toy shop with Shannon last week!" Mom chirps from the main door.

"You summoned her. Say the word 'vibrator' and if she's within three miles, she just appears," I hiss. To be fair, Mom came to my rescue at the sex toy shop. The trauma of seeing Jessica with Declan, then creating a minor traffic catastrophe that thankfully missed being covered on local news, meant I was completely useless by the time we'd reached the store's parking lot.

Instructions memorized, she went in and spent ninety minutes doing a fabulous customer service evaluation of the store, and came out with a lifetime of orgasms in a surprisingly compact shopping bag.

"Look at this puppy! While Shannon was having her breakdown in the garbage-covered car, I was a professional and handled everything for her," Mom announces with glee. She fishes a pink and white vibrator out of her purse.

It is bigger than a compact umbrella.

"Jesus Christ!" Amy screams.

"No, he's the butt plug." Mom pouts. "I didn't have enough in my budget for him."

The three of us stare at him, mouths agape.

Make it four. Even Chuckles' jaw drops just a little.

"They make a Jesus butt plug?" Amanda asks in a shaky voice.

"See why I wanted you to go with her?" I say with more viciousness in my tone than I'd planned. But it's sincere.

"See why I blackmailed you?"

Fair enough.

"Let's go for that walk while Amanda stalks

your ex boyfriend to learn how his mom died," Amy says in a shell-shocked voice.

Mom marches into the living room and searches through the coat closet.

"What are you doing?" Amy asks.

"I need to hide this," Mom announces.

"Oh, God, we don't need to watch that!" I shout.

"Not in my body," Mom says with disgust. "In your closet. It's a surprise for your dad."

"Oh, that would be a surprise in bed, all right. It's basically a third partner."

Mom brightens. "That was my thinking, too!" She frowns. "Why are you researching how someone's mom died?"

"We're making plans," Amy whispers. "His mom came home with a giant vibrator one day and BAM!"

"I heard that." She shoves the vibrator inside a bag with great effort, shoving once, twice, three times.

"Give the poor thing a cigarette after all that," I mutter. "You didn't even buy it dinner."

Mom makes a sour face at me, then brightens as she sees Amanda at the laptop. "Are you really researching how Declan's mother died? Did James do it?" A bit too eager with that question, isn't she?

"Hey, wait a minute. You never finished telling me how Declan nearly became my stepbrother."

Amy does a double take. "What? Wouldn't that make Shannon and Declan's relationship incestuous?"

"No, more like Marcia and Greg on *The Brady Bunch*."

"Ewwww," Amy and Amanda say in unison.

Mom pretends not to hear us.

"Mom? James? You said you dated him."

"When did I say that?"

"The day Steve appeared at the ice cream shop."

She frowns, then grins like an idiot. "You were so commanding with Steve! So fem dom! I'll bet if you got one of those strap-ons at the sex toy shop—it turns out they're not just for lesbians!—you could have…"

Her voice trails off when she sees the looks on our faces.

"Walk!" Amy announces. "You'll spill your guts while Amanda does her cybersearching."

"Where are we walking?"

"Not where. What. The plank." She shoves me out the front door.

The big orange fireball in the sky is so interesting. I haven't seen it for days, holed up in my apartment, and I'm tempted to wave hello, like it's some neighbor I've known for years but haven't chatted with for a long time.

"*Some vibrators are pretty nice*," I taunt Amy. "You had to say that, didn't you?"

"Sometimes it's true." She won't back down. Sheesh. Little sister syndrome. When in doubt, dig in your heels.

"Something is very wrong with you," I mutter, but we go for a walk. Because she's right.

Not about the vibrators, but about needing to get out of the house.

"Tell the story about James, Mom. I can't believe you let a real billionaire get away." She misses the obvious sarcasm in my voice.

She chuckles. It's not a happy sound. "He wasn't a billionaire back then. Far from it. I was an artist's assistant in some crappy squatter's building where we were all avant-garde painters and he was with the real estate company that was trying to turn our run-down warehouse into fancy loft apartments. If he could get the building, he could make his first fortune. Only one thing stopped him."

"You?"

"Rats."

"Rats?"

"Rats." She says that single word like it explains everything.

Chapter Nine

"Go on."

"You want me to go on about rats?"

"Could you please connect the rats to James?"

"Isn't it clear?"

"No."

She sighs heavily. "The building was overrun with rats."

Amy and I both shudder and gag. I shudder, she gags. Then we trade.

"And the only way to keep the rats away was with cats."

"Is that where we got Chuckles?"

She snickers. "No, but Chuckles could be the baby of one of the babies of one of those old warehouse cats. There were so many."

"Rat killer thrice removed," Amy says.

"Get on with it. The James part." I'm impatient. My life is hanging in the balance here. Amanda's researching what the hell happened with Declan's mother, who died in a most fragile way and one that could kill me, too. Meanwhile, my mother spills the fact that she once dated (slept with?) Declan's father, and she's blathering on about rats.

"So when he saw how we controlled the rats, he went to the humane society and adopted fifty cats. Set them loose in the building. Except he didn't think about the stray dogs in the neighborhood."

"Dogs?"

Mom's laugh is infectious, and I study her profile. The years strip off her face and she looks like she's twenty again. Sunshine frames her face and I hold my breath, enraptured.

"All these dogs started sniffing around the building, howling. They wouldn't kill the rats, but they loved to chase the cats. We slept on these little pallets in the art studios and it reached a point where you didn't know if a rat, a cat, or a dog was running over your body at 3 a.m." She makes a funny frowny face. "Or if it was the residual effects of the hit of acid from that night."

"Are you sure any of this is true?" Amy asks. "Maybe it's all just an elaborate flashback."

Mom whacks her lightly on the arm and Amy yelps with manufactured injury. "It's all true. You can ask James."

"I can't ask James anything," I argue.

"Sure you can. He's still your client."

"What about you and him? How'd you start dating?"

"He came to the building one day and was horrified to find that it had become a doggie hotel. The cats were in hiding, the rats were gone, and a ton of homeless women had followed the dogs who were so starved for attention that they curled up in everyone's laps. There was one, named Winky— this cute little mangy Jack Russell terrier. That thing was smaller than some of the rats he managed to kill."

"A rat-killing terrier?" Amy's laughing.

"Mom! Dating!"

"He came over one day to assess the mess and I told him he had to take care of Winky's vet bill. The poor thing had an infected paw from a rat bite. James thought I was crazy."

"You are crazy," Amy and I say in unison.

"James agreed." She chuckles. "I got that man to take me and Winky to a downtown veterinarian who treated him with antibiotics and stitches, though. James paid the bill, then asked me out for dinner."

I stop smiling. "When was this?"

"About a year before he married Elena."

Elena. Mom knows her name. Mom knew all this time about Declan and played dumb. The sidewalk dips and cracks from old tree roots along the tree lawn, and I halt, one foot higher than the other on a slab of concrete. Being off kilter makes sense.

"You've been lying this entire time," I blurt out.

"Not lying, honey."

"Don't call me honey! Declan called me honey!"

"I haven't lied, Shannon. I just…didn't tell you."

"A lie by omission is still a lie." Throwing that in her face gives me a certain satisfaction, because it was what she always said to us when we were kids and didn't tell the whole truth.

She sighs and looks up at the sky. A massive jet leaves contrails that spread out like a zipper opening, white fluff filling in the space.

"You're right. I didn't know how to tell you."

"All this 'marry a billionaire' and 'you can love a rich man as much as you love a poor man' crap has been because you regret being dumped by James McCormick a million years ago?" I snap.

Angry eyes meet mine.

"That's not true."

"How the hell am I supposed to know what's true, Mom? I dated Declan. I brought the man to Easter dinner and you pretended not to know his mother is dead! A woman whose name you know because you dated his dad."

"I had no idea Elena had died! I haven't seen James McCormick in thirty years, Shannon. Aside from the society and business pages of the newspapers."

"And Jessica Coffin's Twitter stream."

Her cheeks pinken. "He's in there sometimes."

I'm so livid that words turn into angry balloons in my head. I march forward, Mom and Amy rushing to keep up. We're halfway around a giant loop we walk in my neighborhood, and if I have to spend one more second being patronized I'm going to scream.

"'Marry a billionaire! Billionaire babies! Farmington wedding!' Jesus, Mom, you're one big, fat hypocrite." I come to such a sudden halt that Amy slams into my back and squeaks.

"Does Dad know you dated him?"

"Of course. Jason's the reason I broke up with him."

Awestruck. I'm awestruck, and Amy looks like she's just been hit by a bolt of lightning. Are we smoking? We should have tendrils of fine white smoke pouring up to meet the jet trails.

"You dumped James McCormick to be with Daddy?" I gasp.

"Well, he wasn't *the* James McCormick back then. He was just an arrogant man who was hungry to make a deal and launch himself in the business world."

A pink flower catches my attention. Then the drip of a lawn sprinkler. A dog barks in the distance once. Then twice. The pneumatic wheeze of a dump truck starting to move after being stopped at a red light fills my ears. This cannot be real. My mother cannot be telling me that—

"You mean he was the equivalent of Steve? Like, the 1980s version of Shannon's ex?" Amy says.

Mom swallows, her hand fluttering at the base of her throat, eyes troubled. "I suppose so. I never thought of it that way, but yes."

I slump against a giant, knotted oak, a triple-truck so gnarled and scarred it looks like it saw combat. "That explains so much."

Mom leans against a shiny patch of pale yellow wood where the bark has been picked clean. Sheared off. "I guess it does. I wanted you and Steve to work out because he reminded me of

James."

"And when I brought Declan home?"

"I wanted that even more."

I snort. "Because it was like reliving James. For you. If I got together with Declan it was James, once removed."

"No!" Mom's face flushes bright red, almost purple, and her eyes turn so angry. All that youth that captured her levity and light in her laughter moments ago is banished, replaced by an outrage I rarely see. "Don't conflate the two. I wanted you to be with Declan because it was immediately apparent from spending ten seconds in both your presences that something very unique is there. The air around you two is charged. You don't see that often."

"You didn't have that with James?"

"No." She blinks, hard, working to control her emotions. This is a side of my mother I've rarely seen. In fact, I've *never* seen this.

"What did you mean Daddy's the reason you broke up with James?" I ask quietly. We resume our walk, talking long strides, measuring our speed. Amy's eyes are alert and perceptive; she's taking it all in without saying much.

Mom looks at the sky again. "You can't choose who you fall in love with."

"And you didn't fall in love with James?"

"I tried." Without elaborating, she lets that hang there. A child flies by on a scooter and we move to get out of his way, the wind whipping through his hair, pure joy on his face as he races his

84

dad, who is on his bike on the road. The dad is pedaling slowly, moderating his pace so his son can win.

We all smile at the sight. Mom's face folds in fastest, though, going somber, her eyes a bit haunted. "I tried," she repeats. "But you can't force yourself to love someone if it's not right."

"And maybe that's what's happening with Declan."

"You're not forcing anything, Shannon," she says, gently touching my arm.

"No—not me. Him. Maybe I really wasn't enough." I let a frustrated sigh burst out of me. "Or I was too much." His words ricochet in my head.

"Do you really believe that?"

We round a corner and watch the dad and son fade out over the big hill we're about to climb.

I can't answer. My mouth has gone dry and my throat aches. So much information. Too much history. Mom dated James? Mom rejected James? Mom watched me bring Declan home and didn't say a word? Was that really out of respect or was there something more?

"How did James take it when you ended your relationship?" I ask, deflecting. I don't want to answer her question.

She gives me a rueful smile. "Not well. James doesn't like to lose."

I laugh so hard I trigger a bunch of dogs behind a fence, their furious barking making me laugh even more. "That's an understatement."

"He didn't have a choice. I chose." Her eyes go

to a place I can't even see, where a love that has lasted more than thirty years lives. Dad's in there somewhere, and he and Mom have their own world where they are each other's sun and moon, orbiting each other.

Amy pipes up finally, as if she's been holding back all along from asking a question that's burning a hole in her head. "Mom?"

"Yes?"

"How did you meet Dad?"

Her smile broadens. "He was the vet tech for Winky."

* * *

When we get back from our walk, two issues are clear:

1. We're still going to eat ice cream.
2. Amanda's struck out.

"I have the best Google skills this side of the Mississippi," she groans. "But there's just this obituary. Not even a mention in the society pages. It's…weird."

We're shoving mouthfuls of sex substitute (and no, not vibrators) into our mouths, my caramel chunks a poor substitute for a man's mouth, but hey, I'll take it, when Mom shouts, "Jessica Coffin!"

I inhale a solid piece of chocolate-covered frozen caramel and the world begins to swirl. Can't breathe. Can't think. I thump my chest and stare, bug-eyed, at Mom.

"Look at Shannon do her *Planet of the Apes* imitation," Mom jokes.

Dark spots fill in the edges of my vision. I seriously cannot breathe, and Mom's face changes as she realizes I'm not making a sound.

Amy jumps up and is across the room in seconds, arms wrapping around me from the back as one thought fills my mind:

Death by chocolate is very, very real.

You take first-aid classes and learn the Heimlich maneuver and wrap your arms around a dummy and pull toward you. You practice on another human being without hurting them. In the seconds between life and death in real life, though, you don't realize how hard you have to pull, the force it takes to dislodge an errant chocolate caramel, or the panic that you feel as blood's cut off from your brain, your entire life in the hands of the baby sister who used to break the heads off your Barbies and roast them on a stick in the fire in the wood stove.

If I'm going to die, there's a certain irony that it's like this and not from a bee sting.

Amy, fortunately, turns out to be as much a hero as Declan, and with one rib-cracking yank the chocolate climbs up my throat, scrapes against the back of my tongue, bounces off the top of my mouth, and flies right into Chuckles' eye, sending him sprawling off the back of the couch and into a wastebasket next to the front door.

A hole in one.

Whoop! I inhale so long and hard it's like the sound a hurt toddler makes as they gear up for a big old outraged cry. Chuckles beats me to it, scratching his way out of the trash can and howling with outrage.

"My God, Shannon, are you okay?" Mom asks, rushing over with a glass of water.

Everyone ignores Chuckles. He marches over to the front door and begins peeing in Mom's purse. My throat is raw and I can't say anything, but a weird hitching sound comes out of me, tears rolling down my face as sweet, blessed air makes its way where the frozen caramel just perched.

"Eye," is all I can manage, pointing at the cat, who is now peeing on Amy's shoe. The new Manolo knockoff.

Amy's studying her hands like they're an Oscar statue. "I can't believe I did that," she whispers. Mom gives her a huge hug and they all watch me, Amanda behind me, her hand on my back with a supportive touch.

Normal respiration resumes. By the time I'm okay, Chuckles has moved on to peeing on a plant, a doorstop painted like a bunny, and someone's stray Target bag filled with dish soap. Equal opportunity sprayer, he is.

He hates everyone equally.

"Jessica Coffin made you choke!" Amanda declares, trying to be funny. She fails.

"Why did you shout her name?" I ask. The words make sense to me, but everyone acts like I just spoke in Farsi.

Somehow, Amy understands what I'm asking and repeats it.

Mom frowns. "We can talk about that later."

"Now," I croak.

"Okay, well…" She really doesn't want to say this. "When you're recovered."

I drink all the water in the glass she's given me, heart slowing down. "Thank you," I say to Amy with as much gratitude as my damaged voice can muster.

"Anytime."

"This makes up for the Barbie," I say in a shorthand only siblings understand.

"Finally!" She throws her hand up like an Olympian winning a gold medal. "It only took fifteen years and near-death!"

"That was my favorite Barbie," I rasp. We share a smile. I inhale deeply and turn to Mom.

"Jessica Coffin?"

Amanda points at Mom. "You're right! Perfect!" The two share a look that goes right over my head.

"Care to share?"

"She's the hoity-toity gossip queen. If anyone knows what happened to Elena, it's her. Or her Mom. They both use gossip like it's currency."

My throat nearly closes up again with the implications of what they're saying. "You want me to go and see Jessica Coffin to pick her brain for the answer to how Declan's mother's death is connected to his dumping me?"

All three of them nod.

"You are all in a folie a deux. A tres," I amend, because all three of them are nuts.

"What's that?" Amy asks.

"It's French for 'batpoop crazy,'" Mom explains.

"You speak French?"

"No. But you're not the first person to use that phrase with me."

"And I won't be the last."

"If you don't see her," Mom threatens, "I will."

I give her a dark look. She's unpredictable enough to do it. The shock of seeing Jessica with Declan in Northampton was bad enough. The woman is pure, social media evil. But Mom and Amanda have a point. If there's some secret, some lynchpin to understanding what Declan's mom's death has to do with his breakup with me, then...

"Give me my phone."

And with that I tweet the only woman in the world who resembles my old Barbie.

Before its head was roasted on a stick.

Chapter Ten

"You told me this would be a bunch of hot men running around covered in mud while scaling wooden walls like they do in Army basic training camp commercials," I grouse as I fill the 1287th paper cup with Gatorade. Amanda is slicing oranges and shoving them into little paper cups that will be summarily squashed by the fists of runners and flung in our faces.

And we have to cheer for those same people.

"Amy said that if we volunteer and hand out rehydration we can go to all the after-event parties and meet cool people," Amanda explains. A bee begins to hover over her hands, lazy and drunk, and I back away slowly.

We're at this 10k running event in downtown Boston, surrounded by a crowd that cheers on the runners. Amy's one of the athletes, and Mom and Dad are somewhere nearby, Dad with a camera so big and old it might have a black cloth you have to drape over it, and Mom's wearing four-inch high heels that scream *I Am So Not a Runner*.

The race is for a charity run to raise money for some medical condition I've forgotten already. The runners shoot through mud runs, climb crazy ropes courses, and engage in a manufactured obstacle course that is carefully cultivated to generate maximum filth and photogenic fun.

I just came to help out because Amy's on my case about turning into one of those women they profile on a cable reality television show, the kind with three hundred dolls in a living museum in their basement, or the woman who grows her fingernails out so long she can pick locks across the street.

"And that's my cue to leave," I say softly. Amanda jerks suddenly at the sight of the bee, and I step backward slowly, sticky hands in the air.

"You have your EpiPen?" she asks, giving me a concerned look.

"Three."

"*Three?*" As if on cue, two more staggering bees come over and give the air around her hands an ominous feel.

"Mom's new thing. And the doctor wrote the prescription out happily." I back away and head toward the building where the runners all register. I know there are volunteer spots in there to help with answering questions, directing people to bathrooms, helping with finding outlets to charge dead mobile phones, and to listen to people complain about everything from the dye in the Gatorade to questions about whether the oranges have GMOs in them.

Ah, Boston. Don't ever change.

I can't avoid bees and wasps in May in New England. Impossible. Unlike Declan's brother, I have no desire to live my entire life in some self-created bubble where I never go outdoors, never feel the sun shine on my skin. Being fully aware and carefully prepared for stings and medical responses is one thing; never taking the tiniest risk and being unable to enjoy the vast majority of what it means to live a rich, fully human life is quite another.

A pang of sadness fills me as I make a beeline (pun intended) for the bathroom. Declan. He was the cornerstone of what I thought would be that kind of life, one filled with fun and hope and love. I set the feeling aside like an errant child who needs to be put on Time-Out. I go to the bank of sinks to wash off the sugar.

The past week has been one long string of rejection, starting with Jessica Coffin, who completely ignored my direct message on Twitter and my carefully worded email through the Contact Us form on her website. Nothing. Nada. My dreams have shifted from sexy times with Declan to pitchforks and torches, Barbie heads on spikes and ogres noshing on jointed Barbie legs.

The new system at work that Josh carefully designed has been spitting back every single report my shoppers submit, and Chuckles hates my guts even more, refusing to sit in my lap after I hocked up a chocolate projectile and gave him the kitty version of a black eye.

I can't win.

Scrubbed clean and no longer a bee or wasp magnet, I walk out to a long hallway and look up to see Declan and his brother, Andrew, standing at the end.

Speak of the queen bee.

Optical illusion, right? My brain created it. They take three steps to the left and disappear, the long white floor making a channel of white light into a tunnel that feeds into a glass-covered wall at the building's exterior. I feel like something out of a movie about death and the afterlife.

Like being reborn.

What would Declan be doing here? It's a Saturday, and we're across the bay. There's no reason for him and his brother to be in this high-rise business building unless...

My eyes scan the walls near the bathroom doors. If I'm right, I'll find it in under a minute. And...yes. "Employees Only."

And next to that door is a small placard that reads:

"Managed By Anterdec Industries."

His company owns this building, and there are five thousand runners and friends using it for the race's headquarters, which means my heart starts to race and my palms sweat, because I am about to see him for the first time since our disastrous last meeting.

All because of a few bees outside.

Maybe Andrew's got it right. What if sealing yourself off from the rest of the world because you know there's one lethal enemy out there that is sociopathic and ready to destroy you with one touch is the right move after all? What if one sigh, one hitched eyebrow, one frown, one dismissive huff could crush you?

Would you do everything in your power to get

away from them—forever?

Reason would dictate that any person of average intelligence and with a little common sense would do so.

Especially my heart. Because while I won't go to his extremes to protect myself from the absolutely random, utterly errant, highly unpredictable sting, I might hermetically seal up my heart because—

This is just too hard.

Suddenly, I understand Declan's brother better. Screw the world—I'll just build a bubble around myself and not even try to justify it. Make the world bend to me. Team Andrew all the way.

I should get some oranges and Gatorade and toss them his way. Maybe a little to the left, though, where Declan's standing.

I walk slowly down the hall toward the sunlight, glad now for my tennis shoes, which make not a single sound on the floor. Two men's voices murmur softly to each other, and I slow down. What a dilemma.

Walk past them and acknowledge their presence, or march on past and pretend I'm not there?

I'm not there.

Notice how I said that? Not pretend *they're* not there. Me. I make myself invisible because I don't know any other way.

"You should say something to her," Andrew says. I freeze. A handful of people run to and fro in the space at the end of the hall, all of them wearing jogger's shorts and carrying clipboards. The leaders are only a few minutes away and I need to go somewhere to help.

Missing this conversation, though, is worth incurring the wrath of Amy.

"Jessica's here. I don't want to add fuel that fire." *Her* is Jessica? Boo. Hiss. She's here? I'll go back outside and risk the bees and wasps to get a giant container of Gatorade and go Belichick on her ass. Pin her down and make her talk, Pry open those Botoxed pork chop lips and—

"You're not dating Jessica, though." *He's not? Whew!*

"And I'm not dating Shannon." *Oh! Oh! So* her *is me!*

"Which is stupid." *TEAM ANDREW! I knew I liked this guy!*

"What? My love life isn't any of your business."

"Following Dad's orders isn't exactly your standard operating procedure, Declan."

James? What the hell does James have to do with Declan's dating me? Orders?

I am sliding against the textured, wallpapered wall like a ninja, but with a rack like mine I resemble a silent warrior mastermind who can make himself seem invisible and discreet about as much as LeBron James resembles Mother Teresa in the humility department.

I try anyway, because eavesdropping on this conversation is the mystery shop of a lifetime.

"Dad didn't make me stop dating Shannon and

you know it damn well, Andrew." A long, slow, angry sigh comes out of Declan, and I can imagine him, even if I can't see him, running a shaky hand through his hair. It's been a month since we've been together and I can't get a good look now. Is his hair growing out a bit from his super-short cut? Does he get it clipped regularly? Does he still smell like—

Andrew laughs, the kind of noise only a sibling can make. "Then you're being even more ridiculous than I thought. Not pissing Dad off is one thing. Dumping the first woman I've ever heard you really fall for is just asinine, and your reason is stupid. Plus, she has a hot friend."

Falling for? Reason? Hot friend? He thinks Amanda's hot? I need to tell her so she can run away from the killer bees and come in here and—

Wait—WHAT REASON? Maybe I don't need to kidnap Jessica after all. I crane my neck, inches away from the end of the hall, now exposing myself to certain discovery but not caring. I have to know. I need to know. He wouldn't tell me when I asked, and now this casual conversation tells me more than anything I've guessed.

"Dad's wrong about plenty of issues, but not this one," Declan says.

"Dec." Andrew's voice is suddenly so pained it makes me pause. Sometimes one syllable can have more emotion in it than one thousand words.

An involuntary sadness fills me. "It wasn't your fault," Andrew continues. *What* wasn't his fault? Our breakup? Because it damn sure was Declan's fault! I didn't dump him in the hallway of

97

his company while Mail Boy rubbernecked with a cart creakier than a rusted Tin Man.

This is one of those moments where blood rushes to my ears, I can count the molecules in my breath, the ceiling seems lower suddenly, and the walls expand as if they seek infinity.

The moment when my life unfolds, for good or for bad.

"You keep saying that," Declan responds. "Been saying it for ten years."

Ten years? He's only known me for a month.

"And I'll say it for rest of my life," Andrew adds. I hear him take a deep breath to say something more, and just when I think I'm about to understand how the world works, how all the gears fit into place to turn the crank and function, why Declan broke up with me, and how maybe—just the tiniest taste of maybe?—I can find my way back to him, I hear:

"Oh. Hello." Declan's voice goes tight. He's clearly talking with someone he didn't expect to see. Did Jessica crash my conversation?

Mine.

Because they're talking about *me*.

"Declan." The voice is low, gravelly, and very angry.

That voice is my dad's. Controlled and tight, he introduces himself to Andrew, whose voice shifts down a half-octave, like a bunch of younger gorillas meeting a new orangutan they've never seen before, but one who disrupts the social order not only because he's strange looking, but because he's communicating pretty clearly that you don't mess with him.

My *dad*. The one who let me paint his toenails pink when I was seven and who walked around at the beach in flip-flops? The former vet tech who stole Mom away from Declan's dad?

Andrew says his goodbyes. *Please don't need to pee. Please don't need to pee. Please don't need to pee*, I pray, and he doesn't turn the corner. If he did, we'd be able to kiss, because my ear is that close to the edge of the hall.

My ex and my dad are about to square off. A rush of heat and terror spikes my skin. If I ever imagined a parent calling Declan out if would be Mom, like she did with Steve at the ice cream parlor. Not...my dad.

"How are you?" Declan asks conversationally. His voice is so neutral it sounds like a series of sound bites, like phone trees at major corporations. How—Are—You? He couldn't sound more robotic if he tried. I've seen him in enough tense situations to know that this is not his normal reaction.

"You don't need to engage in meaningless pleasantries," Dad replies. His voice is so deep, so filled with implied rage. Danger pours out of that mouth, and I'm hearing a side to him I didn't know he possessed.

A long time ago Mom told me something I didn't understand. She said, "Marry a beta-alpha."

"A what?"

"A beta-alpha. It's a kind of man. You know what an alpha male is, right? The dominant, self-assured, slightly arrogant guy who annoys you just enough to hate him but he's so powerful and commanding that against your better judgment you want to sleep with him. Desperately."

"Uh, sure." She'd said this to me right after Steve dumped me, and if I was going to sleep with anyone, it would be Ben & Jerry.

"A beta-alpha is different. He's the man who seems more docile. Whipped, even."

"Like Dad."

She had laughed. "Like your father, but don't ever be fooled, Shannon. Jason is the one in charge when he needs to be. We're equals—always have been, always will be—and he just doesn't care about the trivial stuff like I do."

"Dad has an alpha side? Where does he hide it? In your purse?"

She'd held up one perfectly manicured finger and wagged it in my face, hard. "And that's your mistake. With your father, you can push and push and push and he won't push back until you cross his line. That line is way, way farther back than most men's lines, but it's there."

"A line?"

"You cross a beta-alpha's line and the alpha comes out. And it takes a long, long time to make it go away. And don't ever think that it's lesser just because he's a beta most of the time." She'd given me a long, hard look. "Beta-alphas always, always win."

"Over a what? An alpha-alpha?" I'd snickered.

Her wistful smile had made my heart pause.

"Over every other man who think they have the right to cross the line of anyone your father loves."

I think Declan just found that line.

"Pleasantries." Declan's not asking a question, or requesting clarification. "No."

The abject silence that follows his final word makes me feel like I'm floating to the ceiling, like gravity ceased to exist with that single declaration of "no," like all the laws of physics don't matter any longer, because my father and Declan are facing off over me.

Me.

"Good. I'm not here to yell at you or exact revenge, or"—Dad blows a long puff of air out, and I can imagine him shifting his weight onto one hip, his toes curling under as he struggles with something he doesn't want to face, but makes himself do it anyhow—"but I'm here to tell you that if you broke up with Shannon because of what happened to your mother, then you might want to rethink that."

Your mother? Dad knows what I've been trying to figure out for the past week? It's like God took the world and shook it, hard, like a snow globe.

"Excuse me?"

Dad laughs, not the gentle laugh of my childhood, or the boisterous, rumbling sound of comedy, but a more nuanced sound, one that is masculine and just the tiniest bit dangerous.

"Steve was the last man to hurt Shannon. I never liked him." Dad's voice goes raspy. Confidential. I see his fingers twitch at his hip, as if he's holding back from grabbing Declan's elbow and pulling him in closer to tell a secret.

"Never liked him," Dad continues, eyes narrowing. "I faked it. Pretended he was fine, but there was always something not quite right with him. Slimy. He was a user. The kind of man who views people as fleshbags they manipulate for their own purposes, then chuck aside when they're done."

Declan makes an ambiguous sound in his throat that sounds like Man Code for "go on."

"You, though, are nothing like Steve."

I can hear Declan smile.

"I liked you the moment I met you, and I know Shannon fell for you. Hard. You don't get that in life more than once, you know? That moment when your eyes meet a total stranger's and you realize you're a goner. Done. You just met the love of your life and forever isn't some fantasy people weave to get through reality. It's staring at you over an injured dog."

"Huh?"

Dad laughs again. "Long story. In your case, it was staring at you over a men's room toilet."

Declan snorts.

I can't stand it. Inching slowly, cheek against the wall, I position my eye so Dad comes into view.

Dad's face goes deadly serious so quickly it's like he's rebooted his emotional core. "But maybe I misjudged you. Maybe you're more like your father than I ever imagined."

"What the hell does my father have to do with

anything?"

"I think you damn well know James has a great deal to do with what *you're* doing to Shannon right now. And I can't do a damn thing to stop you, but I won't keep my mouth shut, either."

Their conflict has my heart ricocheting around my ribcage, and I feel like I'm floating as the two men I care about most in the world are going head-to-head. Dad's face is so red he looks like he'll have a heart attack, and Declan's nostrils flare like a bull's.

"You're just like your father," Dad says, delivering the KO punch.

Gravity does, apparently, cease to exist, because I fall over in shock, my body flying forward and out into the lobby, shoulder and knee cracking against the polished floor, my shriek of surprise echoing in the enormous, airy building like a gunshot ricocheting.

I'm on my side and my hip and shoulder are screaming. I look up to find my father, completely dumbfounded, with his jaw hanging so low it's resting next to me like a pillow, offered in shock.

And Declan is smiling.

Chapter Eleven

He can't fake it, no matter how hard he tries to hide the grin that just spontaneously popped on his face, but the smother job he does is pretty damn good.

"Just testing out my Lucille Ball imitation," I say as I roll onto my back, afraid to stand up. This is far less conspicuous than any limp, anyhow.

"Can I step on her, Mommy?" asks a little toddler as his mom drags him by the hand on the way to the bathrooms.

"No." She's dressed in all-white running clothes, and the little boy is wearing nothing but white, too. "You might get dirty," she snaps.

"You must be Jessica Coffin's sister," I call back to her. She ignores me.

Declan's eyes light up, though he doesn't smile. Dad bends down to help me stand up, but I wave him off.

"You two were about to compare penises, so don't let me interrupt you."

I didn't think Dad's jaw could fall open any more, but somehow it does. Half of Declan's mouth inches up with a quirked look, his eyes on me, conflicted but determined at the same time. He looks like a stern headmaster at a girl's prep school, the pinnacle of authority and a role model for how to comport oneself at all times.

Yet just as likely to take the older girls to his office for a spanking when they're naughty.

Parts of me that aren't supposed to be warm right now feel like sunspots. And parts of me that aren't supposed to be wet are. All in front of my father, who is grasping my elbow like he's pulling me out of the rapids on the Colorado River in the middle of a flash flood.

"Shannon!" Dad exclaims, his voice shifting from the dominant fight tone he just used with Declan to the kindly, concerned father tone I know so well. All the information Mom's given me about him and James from thirty years ago swirls around inside, a churn I can't contain. No one can pivot readily from one stance to another, though; his muscles are corded steel underneath his middle-age paunch, and he has a look in his eyes that makes me a little afraid for Declan.

Once that alpha is unleashed...

"Why are you talking about penises, Shannon?" Declan adds, then shakes his head. A fight between two approaches to me and my father is brewing inside him. I can see it. Mr. Cool is trying to win.

Penitheth, I think, but don't say. Then I giggle as I get on my feet, nursing my sore shoulder. Green eyes narrow and he goes somber. Challenging.

Mr. Ass is, apparently, taking over. This is the same guy I saw a month ago. The one who gives no quarter. Dismissive and closed off, he won't be worth talking to.

And then Declan surprises me.

"Jason," he says, turning to offer Dad a hand to shake. The two grip each other like a stripper hanging on to her pole after a high heel breaks. "Good to see you."

Dad is dismissed. His eyes harden, and while he's older and softer, he's not going anywhere. "Good to see you, too, Declan." Both of them look at me for a microsecond and, like synchronized swimmers, cross their arms over their chests, brows lowering, necks tight, mouths set.

Who are these people?

I don't want to hurt my dad's masculinity here, but I also don't want to miss out on the first chance to talk to Declan in what feels like forever. Because my brain shuts down in overwhelmed moments like this, I blurt out the first thing that comes to mind:

"Andrew thinks Amanda is hot?"

Declan lowers his head, biting his lips in that super-sexy way that he thinks is somehow suppressing a laugh but that just succeeds in making me want him even more.

"Eavesdropping? My dad was right."

A flame of fury engulfs me. He's itching to find reasons—really stupid reasons—to make our breakup my fault. So not my fault. Even when it's on fire, my heart beats for him. Damn it. Time to extinguish it with just the right words.

Which are…

Not there. Because I'm so happy to be a few feet from him, to look at him, to have his eyes on me. I can't come back with a retort because there are no retorts. If I say something—anything—right now, it will probably be a string of babble that makes me sound like I'm speaking in tongues at an evangelical revival.

So I just stare at him like Dory the fish. Just keep staring, just keep staring...

And he stares right back.

Dad clears his throat and gives me a look of consideration, the kind of glance you give someone who impresses you. Like he's underestimated me and has reconsidered based on evidence I don't know I've provided.

"I'll leave you two to talk," he announces, and gives me a wink. Have I neutralized the beta-alpha?

Or did Dad just defer to me because he knows he's secure in who he is?

I'm not nervous. Not anxious or worried or scared or—anything. I am present. Here, fully, in the company of Declan.

And ready to talk.

"Your dad was right about which topic?" I ask Declan, who frowns slightly, confused. One hand slips into his pants pocket and the other opens, palm flat against the wall as if he's holding it up.

Propping up the world.

Andrew's words pump through my mind, analysis impossible right here, face to face with Declan. I can't smell him, breathe in his air, watch the movement of his body under his suit and shirt while dissecting what his brother meant moments ago.

All I can do is ask the source and see if he will

reveal any new truths to me.

Then again, why should he? In his mind I'm just the woman who used him for his money and connections.

"What do you mean?" He's being coy. He knows I heard his conversation with Andrew, and instead of tipping his hand he's tipping my heart. Upside down, shaking it like a pickpocket rolling a victim.

"What isn't your fault? What was Andrew talking about? Something happened ten years ago and you're blaming yourself for it."

Blood drains from his face, but he doesn't change expression, eyes hard now, mouth immobile. No answer. No reaction.

Just a silent *no*.

I refuse the no, though, because I've decided that I can do that. Other people have the right to live according to their internal core, and so do I.

So do I.

What I want is equally important, and if someone else has a different opinion then they can express that and instead of living life as one big chain of reactions to other people's reactions, I'm going to act.

Act.

And process it all later.

My hand covers his, the one pushed against the wall. When our skin connects I feel his trembling. A little too good at making the surface look placid, he keeps all the ripples underneath.

He doesn't have to do that with me.

And he doesn't move his hand. If he had, he would drag my heart with it, and right now I can't handle the road rash.

"Declan?" I prod, my voice as tender as can be. "Where have you been?"

His mouth is set in a firm line, tense and unforgiving, but those eyes narrow with a questioning look, reading my face, and then the tension in his jaw lessens, as if a single layer is peeling back.

His lips part, a thin line of white showing between them as they start to form a word, the beginning of a sentence that will break through whatever wall has been built between us.

"Validating myself." He says it with such nuanced dryness that I'm not sure whether to laugh or be offended.

And then—

"You're not supposed to be here," says a woman's cold voice behind me.

It sounds like death.

I turn around.

Close.

A Coffin.

Declan doesn't move his hand. I cling to that single fact. It's all I have, literally, to hold on to right now.

"Here to take out the garbage? Don't you need that weird little car that looks like you're carrying a bowel movement on the roof?" Jessica says with a sneer.

"No," I say, eyes on her, hard as rock. "If I

110

need a piece of crap to do my job," I say, looking her up and down slowly, "I can find one anywhere. Even on Twitter."

Her eyes lock on my hand. The one touching Declan. The one he's not moving.

Hardened again, he stares at me, then lets his glance dart to her. "You interrupted us," he says coldly.

Is he talking to me? No. I interrupted him and his brother, not him and Jessica. Instead of opening my mouth and stammering a nonsensical apology, I inhale slowly, as silently as I can, and just keep my eyes on Declan, pretending Jessica doesn't exist.

Turnabout is fair play.

"The race is ending. We have photo ops to attend to." Her tongue rolls inside her cheek, the movement so masculine it makes her look like Ann Coulter for a moment.

Declan blinks exactly once, but his fingers move just enough to squeeze mine affectionately, grasping me. "I'll be there."

Her eyebrow arches and the look she gives me makes it clear she thinks I deserve my car. "Don't waste your time. We have more important things to attend to."

He makes a small, derisive sound. "The world won't end if I'm not in a picture at the finish line, holding a ribbon."

She looks like she's been slapped.

"When your company donated heavily to support this charity, it meant—"

"I know what it meant." He is iron. Steel.

111

Titanium. But his thumb caresses the back of my hand, and for all his hardness, I turn soft, my insides a twist of silk sheets, my mind airy with a floating feeling that makes it hard to breathe.

"Don't ruin this for everyone, Declan," she challenges.

"You should take your own advice, Jessica," he says, cool as a cucumber. "How's business?"

She storms off in a mumbling fit.

I don't know what to say. He's standing before me, touching me, my hand the center of the universe, his eyes a distant sun. A million questions race through my mind but I can't capture any of them long enough to read them and translate into coherent speech.

A man's shout from near the front door cuts through the air.

"Jesus Christ! Get it out of here!" It's Andrew, backing away toward the elevator.

"It" turns out to be what looks like a fly, but I know it's not.

It's so much more.

Declan's face goes slack again.

"I'm sorry," he says. "I wish this could be different, but my father is right."

And with that, he grips my hand hard, his face filled with regret, then lets go, the hard clap of his shoes on marble like gunshots.

Chapter Twelve

Limping up the steps to my Soviet-bloc business building makes me feel like one of those over-muscled women on the weightlifting team for Belarus. Except I'm limping and whimpering, and I feel like my pectoral and gluteal muscles have been sent to Siberia for re-education.

For the past three weeks—since right after I saw Declan—my life has been a series of gym shops. Forty-seven of them in twenty days, to be exact. That is more than two per day, which equates to screaming quads and exposing more cellulite per hour than you see on a Cape Cod beach in August.

Rumors of ongoing and persistent underperformance by personal trainers at a particular chain of gyms in the area mean I have to pretend to be a new customer who wants to try the "first hour free" promotion. The gyms generally send the least-senior personal trainer to do these jobs, though the one I just left was quite different. I got a seventy-eight-year-old professional female body builder who had more muscle than my dad, Steve, and possibly Declan combined, and whose skin was the color of the old leather armchair in dad's Man Cave.

Smelled like it, too.

Her teeth had gleamed like polished Chiclets

gum and her eyes were remarkably alert and bright for someone born before WWII. No loose skin under the eyes, no bags at all. Her jaw was so muscled she looked like an aging bulldog.

That woman worked me like Jillian Michaels with a group of mouthy teens sent to some Christian re-education camp in Utah. I haven't had my inner thighs quiver like this since...

Declan.

Damn it. I was trying so hard not to think about him, but leave it to my overactive adductor muscles to make him float into my mind. Three weeks have passed without seeing him, hearing from him—and yet he's in my mind, embedded in my skin, deep in my heart.

Still.

I use both hands to physically lift my right leg up the first cement stair. There are nine of them. Nine. As in my legs are screaming "*nein!*" Pain makes me bilingual.

I'm on stair number four when Josh appears next to me. His legs function. He can hop up those stairs like Richard Simmons after drinking five Red Bulls.

"What's wrong?" he asks with glee, knowing damn well why I am limping. We can't pawn any of these gym shops off on him because the assignment requires female guests.

"Not enough fiber in my diet," I mutter.

His face goes blank. "I thought it was all the gym shops you're doing." He snorts. "I know it's not from really good sex."

"At staff meeting today I'm telling Greg he needs to give you the role of supportive father-to-be on all those cord blood bank shops that are coming up."

His pale face makes me grin inside, because Josh can't stand hospitals. "You wouldn't!"

Before I can reply, he puts up a palm and shakes his head sadly, "Actually, you would," he says, leaping up the remaining stairs like Peter Pan and holding the heavy door open for me.

"Thank you. Just stand there for about thirty-seven more minutes and I'll get there."

A strange scuffling sound from behind us makes us both turn. It's Amanda, kicking a box the size of a small ottoman across the parking lot.

"What are you doing?" Josh calls out.

"I no longer have arms," she whines. "Just shredded, noodly appendages."

"Gym shops?" I shout. Using my diaphragm makes the muscles between my ribs hurt. Now it hurts to talk? I need combat pay for this job, I swear.

Josh drops the door handle and runs down the stairs.

"Hey!" I protest.

"*Please*," he calls back. "I could drive to Starbucks and get us all lattes and return and you'll still be on the eighth stair. I can help Amanda."

He's got a point. I feel like a turtle with fibromyalgia.

Josh comes whizzing up the staircase with the box in his hands like he's Superman. Balancing

Amanda's stuff on one arm, he uses the other to hold the door for me.

"Show-off," Amanda and I say in unison. I look at her and gasp.

"What are you wearing?"

She looks like the human embodiment of the coffee bean/piece of excrement on the top of my car.

"Car wash uniform. I have to go and pretend to be a counter employee for the rest of the day."

"With non-functioning arms?"

"That's what I said! Greg's being unreasonable."

"And that's the uniform?" Josh squeaks, laughing. "I haven't seen that much polyester since I watched the movie *Boogie Nights* with my boyfriend."

Amanda and I pause, which isn't hard. "Boyfriend?" We're in stereo.

Josh blushes. "Well, you know—YES! I have a boyfriend!" he squeals.

We all squeal.

Greg opens a window and sticks his head out. "You guys sound like you're replaying that scene from *Deliverance*. You okay?"

"We're just talking about our cars and how much we love driving in tin cans of humiliation," Amanda shouts back.

Thwack. The window snaps shut.

Josh starts to tell us all about Cameron while I make it to the seventh step and realize that Josh— geeky, smart, goofy, socially deficited Josh—has a

116

boyfriend.

And I don't.

Tears prickle at the edges of the soft skin around my eyeballs, taking the immediacy of my aching muscles away from my attention. I inhale slowly through my nose and grasp my leg, pulling it up. Eight. One more stair to go. Just don't cry until

—

Too late.

"You look great!" Josh says as I pull my leg up to reach the top. "All these gym shops are toning you."

"It's all neutral. I'm eating more ice cream to compensate."

"For what?" Amanda snorts. "You'd have to work out thirty-seven hours a day doing CrossFit to make up for the amount of ice cream you're eating."

I'm about to answer but she makes it up the stairs and is right behind me, nudging me with her shoulder. I'm forced to stumble forward and take three steps in a row.

"You look like you could star in *The Walking Dead*."

"You sound like you could star in *Honey Boo Boo*."

"What does that even mean?"

"I was aiming for 'offensive.'"

"You sailed right past it and hit the 'lame' target."

We get to the stairs. No elevator. Josh and Amanda slip past me and I am grateful for the peace. It takes me seventeen minutes to get to the office. I'm late for the staff meeting.

Just as I walk in, I hear Greg say two different sentences:

"Shannon and you can go to the Catch My Vibe store with her mother."

and

"The Fort shop goes to Shannon per James McCormick's instructions, no matter how much you threaten me, Amanda." Greg flinches just enough to show he's worried.

Both freak me out, though not enough to drown out the screaming pain in my legs.

"Wait—what?" I ask. Three faces turn toward me, Amanda's hostile.

"She can barely move!" Amanda argues, gesturing wildly with her head, her arms immobile.

"Pick up your pen and write your name," I say in a quiet voice.

She's been taking glare lessons from Chuckles, I see.

"It's done," Greg announces. "You get your shot later in the summer," he explains to her. She leans down to drink out of a straw someone shoved in her can of diet soda.

As I bend to sit in my chair, I hear my hamstrings snap like a high-tension cord on a crane. *Ping!*

Greg eyes us warily. Josh adjusts Amanda's straw.

"What's wrong with you two?" Greg finally asks, though he sounds about as eager to know the answer as I am to know the specifics of my parents' sex life. And, like me, Greg is about to hear more than he ever imagined.

"I just had more weight swinging in and out between my legs than you could ever imagine," Amanda wails.

All the blood in Greg's face drains out, like low tide during a tsunami, rushing back in so fast that he looks like a big red beet.

"Um, I meant what's wrong *professionally*. I don't need to know about your sex life," he clarifies.

"This *was* for work! That Bulgarian ex-Olympian at the gym on Union Avenue made me do forty-pound kettlebell reps until I couldn't stand it anymore!"

Greg sighs with relief. "*That* kind of weight between your legs!" He's so relieved.

"What did you think I meant?" she demands.

"Never mind," me, Greg, and Josh say.

"I thought you were upset about The Fort."

"I'm upset about that, too," Amanda adds. "But mostly I just want to get laid."

"Don't look at me," Josh says, palms out.

"Or me," Greg murmurs so quietly only I can hear him.

"I think we're swinging away from professionalism," I whisper in her ear.

"It's the damn sex toy shop I did with your mother!"

"Anyone want coffee?" Greg shouts. Josh jumps up with him and they rush out of the room.

"Note to self," I say. "Mention sex life, get free

coffee from men at work."

"Oh, and here," Amanda says, as if uninterrupted. She flails one arm toward her a giant Vera Bradley bag, hands hanging down like a T-rex, ineffectual and useless. Normally I would take pity on her, but I'm kind of enjoying her pain.

After what feels like an hour, she pulls out a water bottle. One of those big, pink-and-white plastic water bottles that…

Has a giant mushroom cap on the end of it, and a Power button.

"Is that a—OH MY GOD, AMANDA!" I scream, shoving the monstrosity out of my way. It falls to the ground and in the impact, the Power button is pushed. A slow vibration rubs against my foot.

"What? It's from the sex toy shop. You act like you've never seen a vibrator before!"

"Not at work! Here! With Greg and Josh around." I've never met a vibrator I didn't like, frankly, but this is a bit much.

"Your mom used part of her product allowance to give this one to you." Mom's been assigned to seven different sex toy shops now because of the way she handled my breakdown in Northampton. Her evaluation was perfect and the client asked for her to do most of the rest of the shops.

I'm so proud. It's like having your mother win the Nobel Peace Prize.

Almost.

I stare at the buzzing monstrosity and I just…I don't…words disappear. The earth implodes. A supernova of nothingness replaces my consciousness. I did not just receive a hand-picked vibrator from my mother. *Nope nope nope.*

"See? It has a 'D' on the tip. Marie wanted it to remind you of Declan."

"Remind me of...what?"

"Plus, the curvature of the letter makes hitting the G-spot easier." She says this the way a home party product specialist might describe a decorative candle.

"Shut up."

"Why are you so hostile?"

"Some product designer actually thought this was a good idea?" I challenge.

"Your mom said the sex toy shop owner told her it was so your man could leave his mark in an intimate place."

"Where? On your *cervix*? That's like being branded! You know a man designed that," I fume.

The vibrator twitches on the ground, but I can't stop it. My legs won't move. I've been sitting here just long enough for atrophy or entropy or oldladykickedmyassery to set in, and all these gym shops have collectively rendered my leg muscles so useless I can't even kick a vibrator with enough power to make it come within range of my hand so I can turn it off.

Bzzzz. "Amanda, can you help me? Reach under there and—"

"Reach? REACH? You ever bench-press eighty pounds, then do ten minutes of high-intensity rowing on a rowing machine while a Bulgarian screams in your ear? I'm lucky my arms are still attached." She looks down. "Okay, good. Still there. Hello, hands. I love you!" She looks up at me. "Just checking."

Bzzzz.

"Greg and Josh will be back any second, and I'd really prefer neither of them has to pick up a vibrator that my mother gave me."

"It's pretty impressive," she says. "Has an anal probe attachment that's shaped like an octopus tentacle."

Greg walks in as she says the end of that sentence. He stops so quickly that hot coffee sloshes out of the tiny sipping holes in the tops of the two take-out cups he carries. His ears perk up and he tilts his head, searching for the sound.

And then his eyes find it.

"Is that a robot vacuum cleaner?" he asks, poking his head under the table to catch a look. "Judy's been mentioning getting one. Says it could really make things better at home, because I've been slacking, and we need something bigger."

"Uh," is all I can say. Just as he bends down, Amanda kicks the vibrator, hard, but her aim is off.

It hits Josh squarely in the shin as he walks in carrying two more coffees. Josh looks down at the bleating white-and-pink flesh penis, then looks at Greg, who has a perplexed look on his walrus-like face.

"That doesn't look like a robot vacuum," Greg says.

Josh is nonplussed by the non sequitur. He

looks at Amanda, then me, and asks:
"Do they make that in purple?"

Chapter Thirteen

No amount of begging, pleading, or offers to clean anyone's shoes with my tongue—including Chuckles'—has made a difference. I am stuck driving my poop-topped car to my mystery shop for The Fort.

Why does this matter, you wonder? Because when you mystery shop a hotel, most clients want a detailed evaluation of every service offered in the hotel. For high-end luxury properties, that begins with valet parking.

That's right. I have to hand off my Turdmobile to a guy who makes more in tips parking Teslas and Ferraris in a day than I make in a week.

And while I'm sure these valets have seen some novel vehicles, including electric-powered Hummers and cars with batwings for doors, a compact car with a big, brown coffee bean that looks like a piece of feces is going to be a new one in their repertoire.

Which throws being inconspicuous out the window.

Even Greg wouldn't relent, making up some sob story about how he needs his car to take his mother to her hip rehab appointment. *Pffft*. Excuses.

The Fort is a massive building of wonder and beauty, blinding in the bright sunshine and shining like a beacon on the edge of Boston's Back Bay. Located right on the edge of all the fun in the city's core, you can walk to fine steakhouses, Faneuil Hall, see the boats come in, go to the aquarium, and have everything at your fingertips.

But first you have to talk to a valet named Guido who looks just like your ex-boyfriend.

Guido—according to the name tag—makes me do a triple take, because if Guido were a few years younger and had green eyes instead of brown, he'd be Declan.

"Holy—*what*?" I exclaim as I climb out of the car, keys in hand. The semicircular covered driveway in front of the glittering bronze-covered entrance seems like it's made of polished marble. As my high heels clack on the ground, I realize it *is* marble. Actual marble.

And because it's just rained, and various car tires have brought water onto the ground, I go flying in the air, keys arcing through the air like they've been ejected from a stomp rocket, arms and legs flailing to grab on to anything so I don't crack my assbone in half.

Two strong hands wrap around my waist and save me from permanent butt damage. The red jacket Guido is wearing unbuttons and reveals a slim waist, broad shoulders stretching the fabric. His hair is a thick, wavy brown like Declan's, eyebrows thicker, a strand of grey here and there peppering his hair. His eyes are kind and worried, though there's a suppressed mirth there, his mouth twitching.

He sets me on my heels, my knee turning inward. I'm dressed in business clothing, the client insisting I assume the role of a C-level female executive traveling for business, in town for the night. And valet parking is the start.

"You hurt?" Guido asks in a bass voice that makes me jolt. If he had poured warm caramel sauce on my nipples I couldn't have had a naughtier response. That voice must get a lot of women out of their pants for him. I, myself, will be using the bathroom clothesline to dry my panties shortly if he speaks again.

"I'm, um, fine," I say, breathless. He steps across from me to retrieve my keys from the ground, giving me a chance to really look at his butt, er...at him. His face. His face! His cheekbones are broader than Declan's, and he's confident in that loose way men who work with their hands for a living have about them.

"Your car?" he asks with arched eyebrows.

"Business car." I smile with more perk than I really feel. I've already developed an excuse for the piece-of-crap car. "Testing a new advertising model for a client."

He nods, like he's in on some joke I don't know about. "I see, Ms.…"

"Jacoby."

"Jacoby." He smiles and gives me a small bow. "Does the market test include aromatherapy as well?"

"What?"

"Never mind, Ms. Jacoby." He jingles my keys

and looks at my car with amusement. More amusement than I've ever felt. "I'll park your company car and keep it safe from harm."

"Really? Actually, I'd prefer you just park it on the street. Maybe someone will steal it and then I'd —" The words are pouring out of my mouth before I can stop them. Something about Guido is so casually comfortable, so companionable, and the facade of being an executive fades away without my even thinking about it.

He smirks and instantly looks nothing like Declan. What was I thinking? I clearly can't get him out of my head, so I'm inventing men who look like him. But when Guido's face goes back to semi-serious, it's like a shadow of my ex is there.

I'm going crazy, aren't I?

Driving the crazy piece of sh—

"I'd lose my job if I did that," he says in a low conspirator's voice.

I swallow, my mouth dry. All the moisture in my body migrates south. "Just kidding."

He eyes me in a way that makes me feel like I felt the first time I ever met Declan.

Inventoried.

"I suspect you aren't. Kidding, that is." And then he just stands there, watching me. It doesn't feel sensual, though. More of a neutral acknowledgement of my existence, for which I'm grateful, because if he starts sending out sexual signals of any kind I'm going to fall over in a puddle of my own goo.

The awkward pause makes me realize he's

waiting for a tip. Of course! We have a mystery shopping procedure for this, so I pull out the $5 bill and hand it to him. He frowns, then glances at the other valets. What kind of parking dude doesn't take the bill and slip it in his pocket with a quick thanks?

My skin starts to tingle. Something doesn't make sense here.

As if I'm handing him a piece of raw steak at a vegan restaurant, he takes the five and puts it in his breast pocket, wincing. Wincing! What kind of guy

—

Oh. Hmmm. Maybe $5 is an insult in a place like this? No one explains tipping guidelines, so staying in an $800-per-night suite might mean that a $5 valet tip—which would be healthy anywhere else—is like pissing on his shoes.

I reach into my purse and pull out a second $5 bill, handing it to him with a smile. "Thank you so much, Guido. Take good care of her."

The other valets laugh and Guido takes my bill with confusion clouding those rich chocolate eyes. "You're giving me more?"

Didn't expect that. "Yes. Is that okay?"

Finally, one of the other valets comes over and taps him on the shoulder. "Dude. Take the money, thank her, and let's go park the piece of—"

I snicker. "We call it the Turdmobile."

Guido laughs, eyes on me the entire time. "You're funny."

If he's flirting, he's horrible at it. But so am I, so maybe the weirdness is me? I can't juggle being "on" for work, doing a mystery shop, and figuring out whether the valet is horrified or attracted to me. Too much input. So I do the simplest thing and just walk away. One step, two step, and down I go—

Splat. *Riiiiiiip.*

I'm showing more ass than J.Lo in a g-string. Guido wasn't there to catch me this time, and I have one leg stretched out with my skirt split so high you can see where Niagara Falls visited my panties.

"Shannon!" Guido calls out, racing to my side.

Now, hold on there. I never told him my first name. But that takes a back seat to the fact that I am staring at the chandelier-topped canopy and a Range Rover the size of my parents' house is about to squish me like a bug.

Guido and his valet friends rush over to me, and four sets of man hands lift me up, making me feel like I'm in one of those romance novels where the woman has more men touching her than she has holes for them to occupy.

"I'm fine," I protest, struggling to control my own body and realizing it's useless. Like synchronized swimmers they set me upright, someone grabbing my carryon and computer bag, another picking up all the items that rolled out when I fell.

Including Mom's vibrator.

"Um," Guido says as he hands it to me. It's the one Mom picked out, with a tip shaped like a J, from the Alphasex Series. The one Josh wants to order in purple. But it's pink, so...

"How did that get in there?" I squeak out, and I'm serious. I have no earthly idea how it got in my laptop bag. Maybe Chuckles is playing an elaborate joke.

A vague memory of Mom in my closet that day after the sex toy shop in Northampton. J?

Oh. My stomach roils.

J for Jason. Mom got me one with a D on it, too. I crane my neck, twisting around, eyes on the ground. Where's that one? If one vibrator magically appears in my bag, I'm sure there are more.

"I've seen some crazy tips before, but..." Guido jokes. I shove the damn vibrator in my bag and decide that the best way to handle this with grace and dignity is to walk away without another word.

"I hope your stay is a pleasant one, Ms. Jacoby! You can believe all the *buzz* about The Fort," he says as I walk away. I swear he winks. And in the recesses of my professional mind I think:

Reminded me to have a pleasant stay? Check.

Sigh.

Chapter Fourteen

Another valet, Mike, removes my luggage from the trunk of my car and escorts me into the lobby. "Lobby" is an understatement.

The first wonder of the modern world is more like it. Grey Industries couldn't come up with something this fine if they tried. I can tell James McCormick has stamped his touch on this place in the most subtle of ways, from the enormous Persian rug that covers a quarter of the lobby to the old world map imprinted in the arched ceiling, a deep cupola made of highly polished oak and bronze highlights screaming with his style. It looks just like his office at Anterdec Insustries.

All of the lights are dimmed, with sunshine from the skylight adding just enough to make the lobby ethereal. I feel like I'm in a steampunk mystery, the blend of old-world flavor and modern technology so exquisite I could be in a slightly different dimension, couldn't I? Just tilted enough to be between two possibilities.

Check-in goes smoothly—Mike disappears with my luggage—and I'm assigned to room 1416, which means climbing into one of the elevators of doom. You know the kind. Major hotels have them. You punch in your floor number and the smart elevator system tells you which one to go on.

Inside, there is no panel of numbers for floors, because the system is designed to assume that you are a pathetic, stupid human with inferior reasoning skills, and that the engineers (almost all male) who designed the system are smarter than you.

Which means that if you get on the elevator and a harassing asshole is on with you, you're stuck in elevator purgatory until the Machine of Superior Intellect decides to spring you out of your misogynistic prison.

I ascend to the fourteenth floor without incident, noting the condition of all the common areas (pristine), then enter my room. The bed is covered with fine chocolates from a Swiss company that uses slave-free chocolate, and the towels are twisted to form a gorgeous rendering of the *Mona Lisa* in 3D.

I plop my carryon on the bed, and the valet has already delivered my rolling bag. One of the first steps I take in any hotel room I enter is to check out the balcony, if there is one. The thick black-out curtains take some serious muscle to pull apart, but the work is worth it. A stunning view of the city rolls out before me. Opening the sliding glass doors, I let the wind whip through my hair and carry my worries away.

A gentle knock at the door compels me to open it. Mike is standing there, smiling. He looks nothing like Guido, and resembles Merry the Hobbit mostly.

"Everything to your liking, Ms. Jacoby?"

I know the drill. I slip him a five and assure him all is well. He tips his hat to me and walks

134

calmly down the hall.

My nineteen-page (*nineteen*-page!) list of instructions for the twenty-seven-page evaluation tells me exactly what to do for the night I'm here. If you mystery shop a lower-market chain of hotels you typically get your room free, about $25 in pay, and reimbursement for one dinner and a tip for housekeeping.

This place involves:

Valet parking
Tipping the bellhop
Drinks in the bar (two, minimum)
A full dinner from room service, from appetizer to entree to dessert
Breakfast buffet in the morning
Housekeeping tip
A massage in the spa
Tipping the bellhop on check out
Valet parking tip upon checkout

This is how the other half lives? If so, how do I join them?

But that's not all.

Like relationships, you learn way more about customer service by testing them via problems. Any hotel or restaurant can run smoothly when it's quiet, when they're fully staffed, and when nothing's gone wrong.

The true test of a business is how its employees react to crisis.

Even manufactured crisis.

And my job is to manufacture a series of them, starting with the bathroom. I read the instructions, which were written by Amanda:

Facilities and Engineering: Create a problem with a fixture in the bathroom, a problem great enough to require a service call from one of our facilities workers. For instance, separate the chain from the ball in the toilet tank, or remove the nut that secures to one of the bolts on the underside of the toilet seat. Tuck the loose nut under the wastebasket.

The goal is to test the friendliness of the front-desk clerk, the response time of the facilities worker, and whether their service is friendly and efficient.

Okay. Standard operating procedure for a hotel mystery shop. I've done this tons of times before. My old standby is a little more creative than these suggestions, for I typically just make it so the toilet handle doesn't connect to the flushing mechanism.

Easy peasy.

I make the call first, eager to get this out of the way so I can move on to drinking at the bar...er, to the next task for my job. The hotel has an ice bar—an entire nightclub carved out of ice. The hotel desk clerk (Celeste) takes my call in stride, apologizes for the inconvenience, and at 3:56 p.m. promises that someone from their maintenance department will respond within ten minutes.

Great. I have ten minutes to break something. I'm Shannon; how hard can *that* be?

Something buzzes in the next room. My phone.
I search the room and my eyes locate it, but it's not
lit up. No text.

Bzzzzz.

Weird. What could be buzzing like that?

My carryon starts to move of its own accord,
edging toward the end of the bed. I open it and—

A giant, carved J stares at me. It's pink.

Oh, yes.

Mom's Special Surprise.

The Power button appears to be jammed, and
no matter how hard I try, I can't get it to pop up and
stop vibrating. My fingers worry the little button,
and in frustration I bang it—hard—against the edge
of the desk.

BZZZZZZZZZZZ.

I appear to have whacked it into hyperdrive. If
it were the Millennium Falcon then Chewbacca
would be turning all the thrusters on for Han Solo.

That sounds *soooo* dirty.

The vibrator is buzzing so loudly I'm sure the
people in 1414 can hear it loud and clear. Removing
the batteries should do the trick. I turn the cylinder
over and—

Screwdriver needed.

Damn.

Tap tap tap. Someone's at the door.

"Maintenance!" a man's voice calls out.

I look at the clock. 3:58 p.m. Great. Of all the
times for me to get the overachieving hotel
maintenance dude. The only one on the freaking
planet. I race into the bathroom and shove the top of

137

the toilet tank off with one hand. Not being strong enough, I set the vibrator on the counter.

BZZZZZZZZ. That only amplifies the sound.

Tap tap tap.

"Ma'am? It's maintenance. The front desk sent me," he says, a little louder. His voice is muffled and my hearing is slightly obscured by the rush of panic that makes the room start to spin. I break into a sweat as I grab the vibrator to stop the roaring sound and reach inside the toilet tank to loosen the chain from the handle. In mere seconds, I manage to do it, but as I stand up from my crouch I lose my balance and—

Splash!

Drop the giant pink vibrator into the toilet.

The J stares up at me, a bit of a blur as it motorboats inside the bowl.

The distinct sound of the electronic key being shoved in the slot of my door happens in slow motion, the sound like a series of guns in a firing squad being loaded, then locked on me.

I crouch down again and shove my hand into the tank to grab the vibrator, scanning the room for something I can use to mute it. Snatch it out of the toilet and wrap it in a towel? Maybe. Best plan I have.

But the door to my room opens and a familiar man's voice calls out.

"Hello?"

"I'm, uh…" I try to kick the door closed to buy time, but all I accomplish is a slow slide on the tile in my heels, my skirt dragging up to show the edge of my panties. I'm elbow deep in the toilet bowl, my hand smothering my mother's sex trophy meant for my *dad*.

And then a very familiar face appears with two highly amused, sparkling green eyes.

He looks at me, eyes scanning my half-acre of leg and thigh, my arm buried in the toilet, and says:

"We have *got* to stop meeting like this."

Chapter Fifteen

Declan's face, his eyes, his voice, that saucy grin do not compute with the blue workman's shirt he's wearing. Red embroidery on a yellow name tag says Alfred, and he's wearing Dickies work pants with tan construction worker's boots.

He looks like any generic guy from my neighborhood back home. Like the dads of my friends. Like my male friends grown up now, in their early twenties, working in auto shops and framing houses.

"Layoffs at Anterdec got you working with your hands?" I say, leaning against the toilet bowl like it's all good. Casual. Nothing to see here. Just drowning a sex toy to put it out of its misery.

"I thought I'd develop a new skill to fall back on." He cocks one eyebrow and leans forward to see what I'm doing. "You drop your phone again?"

"Yep!" I chirp. "Sure did! Silly me, you know how I—"

Ring!

I changed my ringtone to that antiquated tone that sounds like a rotary phone.

Clearing his throat, he states the obvious because hey, that's what you do when you corner a woman who is insane: "Your phone is ringing."

"I'm not exactly going to answer it like this,

now, am I?" I snap.

"Why don't you get up and...hmmm," he says, assessing the situation. His head turns to look in the room, then over my legs at the toilet, hands planted on his hips as he judges the situation and determines that there's something wrong with finding me in a compromising position with the toilet.

"Are you drowning a tiny pink pig in the toilet?"

"Science experiment!"

Ring!

Does he have to look so damn hot while he's dragging out this moment of impending humiliation and doom? It's bad enough to be caught with my hand in the toilet—again!—but this time I'll pull out my mom's battery-operated boyfriend and go through the triple embarrassment of being turned on by the tight hang of his work outfit along his hips, how the cloth contours to those muscled thighs, the way the shirt is unbuttoned just enough to show his sprinkling of chest hair, and how the short sleeves showcase biceps that used to slide under my body and prop me up for his mouth as he—

Grabs my arm and pulls it out, dripping and buzzing from a gasping sex toy.

"You were drowning a...*that*? What the hell *is* that? A Barbie doll?"

I toss it at him. What do I have to lose at this point?

He sidesteps it neatly and it lands on the rug, turning to the left like a drunk driving in a roundabout.

"Definitely not a Barbie doll," he says, laughing.

"I stopped playing with those a long time ago," I say.

"I see you still have your favorite toys, though," Declan replies. "And why a 'J' on the tip? No 'D'?" he says, leering.

All I can do is glare. My heart is buzzing in my chest like a—well, you know—and he's looking at me like I'm a human being again. Like he likes me. Like he actually wants to interact with me.

"Why are you here?" I demand.

"The front-desk clerk said the toilet was broken." He holds up a small toolkit. "We have a completely different set of tools for malfunctioning vibrators."

"There's a protocol for *that*?" I gasp. Wow. And I thought I'd seen it all as a mystery shopper.

He nods and says dryly, "Yes. We just grab an EpiPen and shove it in there as hard as possible."

My turn to size him up. I'm standing here with a dripping arm (again), toilet water soaking my sleeve (again), and Declan's in disguise like he's dressed up as a superintendent for some very pervy Halloween party.

"Why are *you* answering my maintenance call?"

He seems surprised to be asked. "Amanda didn't coordinate this with you?"

"Amanda?" I say dumbly. "*Amanda* Amanda?"

"Is that really her last name? Cruel parents," he says with a low whistle.

"No, her last name is not—quit changing the subject!" I demand, turning away. My jacket is ruined, so I slide out of it to review the current state of my clothing. White silk business shirt—one arm wet. Jacket wrinkling rapidly on the floor—needs to be dry-cleaned.

Suit skirt split just like the first date—business dinner—whatever you call it.

My life is one big repeat, isn't it?

And here I am, all twitterpated because the ex-boyfriend who inexplicably dumped me is giving me some attention.

My life is one endless loop.

I can stop this, though. I can make choices that don't let other people do this—whatever this is—to me. Declan thinks he can waltz in to my hotel room dressed in uniform and smile and make me go weak in the knees and I'm just going to take the table scraps he's throwing my way like a good little doggie.

Ruff ruff.

"Why are you dressed in that uniform and responding to my service call?" I demand again.

"Because Amanda suggested that as part of measuring and following customer service standards to aid in marketing pushes with conventions, I perform some small version of that reality TV show, *Meet the Hidden Boss*, and go undercover in my own company's property."

I frown. "Didn't some CEO here in Boston do that recently?"

He nods. "Mike Bournham."

144

Bournham. Playboy. A sex tape that went viral. Something about a poor, naïve administrative assistant.

Utter disgrace and a resignation from him.

"That went *soooo* well for him, didn't it," I say with as much sarcasm as I can.

Declan shrugs. "Amanda was convincing."

I get the feeling she didn't have to push much. A flicker of emotion in his eyes shifts the tenor of the room, the bathroom instantly small in the blink of an eye. I'm washing my arm now—both arms—and all I want to do is get him out of my room so I can take a shower and cry.

BZZZZZZZ. As if reanimated by Dr. Frankenstein himself, the damn vibrator goes into high gear. I stomp across the bathroom, nudge Declan aside, and kick the damn thing as hard as I can.

When I was in middle school, for three years, I played goalie for my soccer team. Haven't done anything more athletic than that in a decade, but my feet must remember how to point the toe and scoop up for a serious drop kick, because that vibrator catches my toe and grabs some serious vault and air, sailing across the room, high over the bed, and flying through the open sliding glass doors, over the balcony railing and—

Down fourteen stories into the street.

We can hear the screech of tires and men shouting, then a few blares of horns.

Declan and I must look like a pair of owls, eyes wide and blinking.

145

I am speechless.

Declan's not.

"Good that you don't have a dog."

"Huh?"

"Because that could have been one game of fetch gone terribly, terribly wrong."

"You're making sick jokes after that just happened?" I point to the balcony. People are screaming at each other in the distance.

"Is there a more appropriate time to make sick jokes?"

"Why are you here?" I demand in a voice with more munition in it than I thought possible. I'm shaking with overwhelm, adrenaline, embarrassment, and excitement.

He starts to answer me. Repeatedly. Four times, in fact. I count each one, and with each new false start I feel a tiny rosebud, tight and contained, start to unfold inside me. One millimeter.

Just one tiny budge.

"I told you," he says in a rush, clearly flustered now, arms crossed over his chest, eyes hooded again. His hair is longer—like in my dream, but still fairly short. Not the rakish, hedonistic man I conjured in my subconscious. In my bed.

Bed.

My eyes flick over to the enormous king bed in the middle of my room, covered in more pillows than a sultan's sex den.

Declan's eyes follow mine. His arms drop. He blinks rapidly, focused on me now entirely, still maddening. Still not answering.

"Surely you haven't changed your name to Alfredo and taken up plumbing," I joke, regretting the intrusion instantly.

He gives me a wan smile. "Maybe I've become a mystery shopper."

I shrug, trying to hide how my heart is trying to break free and go hug his. "I've worn plenty of uniforms before during evals. You wouldn't be unique."

"So I'm not special?"

I measure my answer carefully as a cloud of calm coats me. He's here, and I want him so much, but I can't bridge that gap without an apology. Or even an explanation. Letting men waltz back into my life and resume as if there aren't pieces of broken, bloody glass made up of my soul isn't working for me lately.

Isn't working for me *ever*.

"If you mean are you like all the other men I've dated? No."

He flinches, guarded eyes showing a series of quick snapshots of hurt, confusion, atonement.

"No? I'm on par with *Steve*?" He says his name like a curse word.

I can't do this. I cannot have this conversation with Declan right here, right now. Who does he think he is? My mind scrambles to come up with a pithy comeback, witty repartees that will make him regret what he's cast aside, but instead I fall back on the one approach that comforts me most. That makes me feel real.

The truth.

"What are you doing, Declan? I'm not playing games with you. I don't play games. You chose to break up with me because you didn't know who the 'real' Shannon is. Because you thought I was using you to get ahead in business. Because—"

"Because I'm an idiot," he interrupts, taking one resolute step forward, bridging the gap between us by half. A thick gust of wind billows the stiff curtains inward, the sun flashing off some piece of glass on the desk, and the scent of seawater, the rush of cool air makes the moment seem so ripe with possibility.

"Idiot?"

"Idiot."

One more step. *Please take one more step*, I think. The Shannon inside me that knows I can't be walked all over is fighting with the part that wants him to kiss me, that wants to lose myself in his touch, our lips, a joining of bodies that banishes the clashing of minds.

Does it have to be either/or?

Declan's own struggle is reflected in his eyes, one strong hand moving to his hip, the other reaching up to push through hair I wish I could stroke. I still don't understand what happened a month ago in the hallway outside that meeting. Probably will never understand. But if he could just give me one reason, one tiny sliver of—

And now he's kissing me.

Good reason.

Very good reason. I arch into him, absorbing his warmth, lips parting to let him taste me. As my body softens against him I feel the pull of my heart toward his, like a magnet gathering iron shavings, as if his touch could summon the disparate parts of me and bring them together, whole.

Yes, with just one kiss. And then another. And another, until there is no separation between them. No divide, no marking point where one warm, soft sigh and brush of a tongue and an eager embrace begins and ends. They all blur together, like seconds blur into minutes, minutes into hours, hours and days into the woven cloth of a life well lived.

And loved.

He smells so nice, like Declan. His own branded scent, like tasting him in the air. Hot, eager hands pull me to him like he's planning never to let me go, and the rush of being so close, so deliciously close to him doesn't subside when it should.

If this were a movie, I'd pull back, smack his face, and he'd yank me close and kiss me again.

But this isn't a movie. And he still has not answered my question.

I pull back, the kiss lingering on my mouth like a layer of silk as I ask, "You broke up with me because of your mother, didn't you?"

Another kiss replaces his answer. I slide my hands around his waist and there is this one spot where his shirt has pulled up just enough from his waistband to give me a glorious inch of hot, taut skin to touch, my thumb caressing it, my palm wanting so much more. Bold now, my fingers track upwards along the ropy muscles that parallel his spine, feeling the power of his shoulders as his arms envelop me.

Damn it. He did it again.

Breathless, I pull away just as he steps forward, pushing me gently until the backs of my calves hit the bed. I want to bend. Oh, how my knees want to fold just enough to sink us both into the down-filled duvet, to wake up in the morning with pillow mint wrappers stuck in my hair, and not because I ate a bag of them alone while watching the first episode of *Outlander* repeatedly and crying about how there are no good men like Jamie.

"No," I whisper, making him look at me. "Not yet. You can't waltz in here like this and expect me to let you pick up where we left off, because you left off in a spectacularly crappy way."

He pinches the bridge of his nose and steps back, warm breath coming out in waves as he fights to control his panting. "Yes. You're right."

"That's a good start," I mumble. The United States of Shannon is a federation of states all working together, but a few parts of me—all below the waist—are calling constitutional conventions to discuss secession.

Traitors.

"Are you going to listen to me, or just crack wise?" Declan asks in a tight voice.

Record-scratch moment. *Screech!* Hold on.

"If you're here because you want to get back together, you have some explaining to do," I say, ignoring my clitoris, which is attempting to call the secession meeting to order for a vote. Man, is it banging that gavel. Hard.

150

"So do you."

"Me? What do I have to explain? I tried to explain. No, I never wanted you for your money or for business contracts. No, I'm not a lesbian. Yes, I have a bee allergy. What else do you need to know? Those are all parts of the very real Shannon who is standing right in front of you."

He points a finger at me.

"Don't muddy the waters. The problem is that you took what could have been a simple situation and twisted it into Gordian knot-like complexity," he says in a matter-of-fact tone.

I have no desire in this exact moment to admit that I have no idea what a Gordian knot is, so I say, "How did I make it complicated?"

"You caught Jessica's attention. Anytime she tweets about someone it has to have triggered a rash of rumors so strong it gets back to her," he declares.

"That's my relationship crime? That my ex's ex who is hot for your rod tweeted about my pretending to be gay? You broke up with me for that?" I laugh. I'm genuinely not upset, because that explanation is so freaking lame that I know it's not true.

"No."

"Then why?"

"Because you never bothered to tell me about your allergy."

"It was our *second* date! Don't you think you're being a bit unreasonable? Allergies aren't a second-date thing."

"Second-date thing?"

"You know, kiss on the first date, show your student loan debt on the second, intercourse on the third. There's a timetable for these things. Deathly anaphylactic bee allergy isn't slated until date number seven, filed under Batpoop Crazy Relatives and Genetic Predispositions to Hammertoes."

Peering intently at me, he ponders this. I can tell he's debating, his eyes moving rapidly even open, his teeth sinking into the soft inner flesh of his lip. I've made a cogent point and he has to either react with reason or—

"Not good enough."

Assholery.

"Not good enough? You get to unilaterally declare my explanation 'not good enough'?"

"Yes."

Chapter Sixteen

"No!" I blurt the word out and whip around, grabbing the mints on the pillow and unwrapping them. The erstwhile wrapper goes flying near the wastebasket, wafting down as I shove the chocolate in my mouth, fuming at him.

"Cute. We can argue and shout 'yes' and 'no' at each other all day, Shannon, but you have to admit to yourself that—"

"I remind you of your mother, who died from a wasp sting, and you can't handle that." In finishing his sentence for him I've chosen a path that leads either to the end of everything between us, or a real beginning.

Real.

"Who told you that?"

"Google." I let the tension release from my shoulders. "I'm sorry."

"What else did you read?" His voice is so tight he could string a guitar with it.

"There isn't anything more," I answer, bewildered. "No matter how hard I tried, I couldn't dig anything else up. And Jessica was of no help."

"Jessica?" His carefully constructed facade begins to crack, his face betraying him as he starts to show a few slivers of emotion beyond desire. "What the hell does Jessica have to do with my mother?"

The whole scheme sounds ridiculous now, but I figure I should share. "We thought because she's a gossip girl, she might know what happened ten years ago, so I asked her. Got no response whatsoever. I guess she doesn't know."

"No. She knows what happened. Her non-reply is because she can't stand you."

Nice. At least he's being truthful.

"Then why can't you just tell *me*, Declan?" I ask in a quiet voice. "You've told Jessica. But not me? This obviously has a lot to do with us."

"Us?" The second that syllable is out of his mouth I deconstruct it, finding 17 different meanings when you include vocal inflection, tone, and pacing. "And I never told Jessica," he says with a growl. "She found it out on her own and confronted me with it."

"Confronted?" What is the big secret?

He storms away from me, onto the balcony, bracing his arms on the railing, leaning into the wrought iron in a way that makes his arm muscles bulge, his shoulders spread. Tipping his head down as I join him, he can't—won't—meet my eyes.

I touch him, my hand on his shoulder. He twitches just enough to make me remove it.

"Are you sure you're safe out here?" he asks in a flat voice.

"Safe from what? Flying vibrators?"

He laughs, clearly against his will. Yet he won't look at me. His gaze shifts to the water, eyes tracking a sailboat that glides smoothly on the

154

waves.

"No. From a bee sting."

Anger pours into me like it's been attached to an IV drip bag and administered as medicine. "You can't let it go, can you?"

His head snaps up. "What?"

"You can't let go of the fact that I have this...thing. This allergy. This curse." I feel the rant coiled deep inside, ready to unfurl. "It's not like I have a choice. I didn't ask for this. It's part of who I am, and I take every precaution imaginable—"

"Not every precaution."

I tilt my head and stare at his profile. Red dots of fire kiss my cheeks. Blood courses through me like a tsunami.

This? This is what's stopping him?

"You liar," I spit out.

His eyes light up with a mixture of confusion and indignation.

"Liar?"

"Yes. Liar. You lied to me a month ago. You told me that you thought I was a chameleon, that I wouldn't reveal the real Shannon."

"What does that have to do with my lying about—"

"*This* is the real Shannon. The *real* Shannon can die if she's stung by a bee. The *real* Shannon has boobs that touch the bed when she lies on her back. The *real* Shannon needs to wear spanx to fit into a comfortable size sixteen. The *real* Shannon hates Transformers movies. The *real* Shannon thinks Jessica and Steve and your father and fake people who have overinflated egos and are out of touch with reality."

He isn't showing even the tiniest hint of emotion as he listens, expressionless. His hands are tight fists, though, held close to his thighs, and his nostrils flare as he breathes silently. No reaction.

Oh, yeah? I'll make you react.

"And the *real* Shannon thinks you're a total emotional wuss for thinking that hiding your emotions makes you more of a man," I add. A parting shot, if you will. I want to kiss him again and knock some sense into that handsome face, using my tongue and hands and heart if I have to, but I see, now, that it's no use. He's clinging to his secret and if he won't tell me what's going on, I can't keep playing this game.

My heart isn't a toy.

And with that I storm out of my own room, snatching my purse and instruction sheet.

It's time to evaluate the bar.

* * *

It's an icehouse in here.

This time—literally. I'm fuming and so red-hot on fire that as I walk into the carved-ice bar I fear I'll melt the entire place down with my very presence.

As I step into the sculpted ice room, I realize it's like a cave. The bar has barstools—made of ice. The bar itself is one round-edged sheet of ice.

156

Shelves? Ice.

It's magical.

My nipples tighten from the cold and I look down. All I'm wearing is the thin white silk shirt I have on, the one that got wet a few minutes ago. My soaked sleeve is like a frosted blanket, and I can see my own breath as I exhale. My jacket is back in my room (with Declan) and my skirt is split up to my panty line.

No wonder the girls just went tight and high. It's *cold* in here.

I don't care. My mind can't stop spilling over with a thousand words, most of them profanity-laced diatribes about Declan.

How dare he?

How *dare* he!

Show up and interrupt the most important job I've ever had, mock my profession by pretending to be a maintenance man (yeah, right...like Amanda put him up to it!) and then have the audacity to kiss me. A lot. And then blame me for not telling me what on earth his dead mother has to do with his dumping me!

I need a scotch. Bad.

I sit down gingerly on the cold, hard, ice-topped bar stool. The bartender's back is to me, and he's whistling some tune I don't recognize. The lighting in the bar is a series of cool blue LED bulbs carved into the ice. The entire room is like something out of the set of a new Star Trek film.

The music is soft jazz with a jaunty, bluesy tone to it. The kind of music that gets you warmed up to go to bed with someone. To throw inhibitions into the wind and let your impulses carry you to a new place.

Like a hotel room upstairs.

My skin tingles from the rush of emotion that clings to me, my lips raw from those kisses, my heart shredded and beating like it holds time itself together. Like my heart is responsible for the counting of seconds that pass.

Tick. Tick. Tick. Tick.

That's too big a burden.

Need to drown it in alcohol.

I clear my throat. "Excuse me? Could I order a —" As the bartender turns around and I get a look at his face, I cut my own words off.

It's Andrew.

Declan's brother.

"What are *you* doing here?" I ask, incredulous. A few heads, all male, turn toward the sound of my fairly-loud, and quite demanding, voice. They turn back to their drinks and conversation when Andrew leans in toward me and puts his hand over mine, like we're old friends.

Where Declan is dark and intense, Andrew is fair and blank. Generic. Now that I've seen pictures of their mother, I understand who Andrew takes after. He's not quite blonde, and the eyes are pale brown, like a fine whisky. The broad planes of his face are Declan's, though.

"Would you keep your voice down? When you go undercover you're supposed to blend in."

"I'm blending in!"

"I meant me. I'm acting, and this is my first time, so don't blow it." He's mocking me, pretending to be serious. "I don't want to have to pretend to be a lesbian and have that blow up in my face," he adds.

"You're an asshole."

"Nice language."

"Wait until I have my two drinks in me."

That makes his face crack open in a smile and he sweeps an arm toward the myriad bottles on shelves in front of a highly-polished ice wall. "How may I serve you?"

"Two fingers of scotch. Neat." I've heard my dad order this way at fine bars, so why not?

He pours about two big shots into a tumbler and slides it to me.

I take a sip. The burning feeling does not square with the ice cold chamber I'm in, so I decide to go all-in and just chug it, slamming the glass down on the bar.

"That's it? Two warm shots in a glass?" I gasp as the liquid feels like lighter fluid pouring into my belly button.

"That's what you ordered. Want a wine cooler next time? Or a drink with an umbrella in a coconut?"

I glare at him. "Anything that might attract the attention of a bee would be great."

His eyes go cold, but he looks around the room, then says, "Not in here."

"Not anywhere in your life, so I've been told."

"Dec never was good at keeping his big mouth

shut," Andrew shoots back, which makes me snort in surprise. If Declan's too talkative about, well, anything, then what kind of family did they grow up in? The handful of sentences I can pry out of him about his feelings, his past, his mother are the exact opposite of what Andrew's saying. As the alcohol hits me and fills me with a loose sense of curiosity, I decide that alienating the one person who might give me some insight into Declan McCormick might be a mistake.

A big one.

"He's pretty good at keeping his own secrets close to the vest," I say in a conspirator's voice.

Bingo!

Andrew leans in. "Yes, he is." This gives me a chance to get a good look at him. He's wearing a white, collared shirt, a black vest, and a name tag that says "Jordan."

"Why are you and Declan pretending to work here?" I ask. Not the original question on the tip of my tongue, but right now I'm feeling all squiggly and casual with him. Aside from staring across a board room table at him and hearing about his OCD-crafted life to avoid being stung by a bee, I know nothing about Andrew.

"Your friend set it up. Amanda." His lips spread in an instantaneous smile that he tries to turn into friendliness as her name pours over his lips, but I'm not deceived. Two questions fight for positioning in me, and the one that wins is:

"Amanda?" I cough out her name.

Brilliant, right?

Andrew pours two more shots in my glass and stares at me, hard. My eyes struggle in the dim light to find Declan in him, but all traces are gone.

Another patron at the bar flags for his attention, and he shrugs an apology, leaving me for a minute to pour a requested Guinness. I sip gingerly from the tumbler and remind myself that this is a job. I am working. My smartphone comes in handy and I pull it out, retrieving the evaluation form from my app and as Andrew helps a second customer with a martini, I answer questions with the background noise of the shaker.

"You look like Princess Elsa," a slurry voice says to my right.

I look up, disoriented, and find the face of a man about ten years older than my dad. He's bald, wearing stylish glasses with a black line straight across the top of the lenses, and has an earring in his right ear. Tattoos cover his forearms and he's wearing a plaid button down. It's like L. L. Bean, Mr. Clean and Keith Richards climbed into a Vita Mix and got poured out into a Man Mold.

"You're hitting on me by using Disney movie characters in your pick up line?" I answer, trying to summon outrage as I tuck my smartphone back into my purse. None appears. The whisky just makes me find this all amusing.

My skirt melted part of my bar stool and as I shift, the cloth stays put. My thigh, though, decides to give the female equivalent of The Full Monty. Good thing I'm wearing underpants.

He lifts one shoulder and smiles, revealing two

gold teeth. Both canines. "Can't blame a guy for trying. Great line in a bar made of ice. You got a room here? And a sister?"

"A sister? Why, you have a friend for her?"

"No." His hungry eyes are trying to tell me something, and as I sip my scotch I try to figure it out.

Can't.

"Pete, get the hell out of here," Andrew growls, reappearing quickly. "Quit hitting on people who graduated high school in the twenty-first century. And stop suggesting threesomes."

"She's legal. You're legal, right?"

I'm flattered he might think otherwise, but I'm also trying to process what Andrew just said. Threesomes? "If you think I look like I'm under eighteen, Pete, then you need to get those glasses checked," is all I can think to say.

Andrew hands him a glass of something clear on the rocks. "Go find someone else to bother."

"She yours?" Pete barks out, rotating his look between me and Andrew. "Lucky man. You get those thighs wrapped around your head and you couldn't hear a tornado coming even if it plowed through your building."

I don't have a brother. Don't have a brother-in-law any more. So the look on Andrew's face doesn't make sense to me in the moment, though in later years I'll come to understand it better.

"Get the hell out of here," Andrew says, eyes flicking up to get the attention of the plainclothes security dude at the main door. His name is Jerry (I

162

checked when I walked in) and Jerry's there in three seconds.

"I'm a paying customer," Pete slurs, loose eyes taking me in as I try—and fail—to cover my legs. "Who's your boss? I'll have you fired."

"*I'm* my boss," Andrew says as Jerry escorts (drags) Pete out.

Compassion and a kind of wariness coexist in Andrew's eyes as he looks at me, but seems to struggle to make eye contact at the same time. "You okay?"

He seems more upset than I am. "Me? Yeah. Sure. He's just another asshole man who hits on women." The thigh comment rings through my mind. I don't know whether to be offended or flattered.

Andrew's mouth hangs open a bit. Oh. I guess I said that part aloud.

"Would you be offended?" I add, drinking the rest of my second scotch. "If someone said that about your thighs?" I pull out my phone, not waiting for an answer. "Let me ask Amanda. I wonder if her thighs are big enough to block out sound when she's—"

Andrew turns bright red at the mention of Amanda's name.

Aha.

"Amanda," I say.

Red.

"Amanda!"

He flushes again.

"Oh, this is fun."

"What is?" he asks. "Talking about women's thighs?"

"How about *Amanda's* thighs?"

Red.

"It's warm in here," he mumbles. "Need to turn down the temperature or the ice will melt."

"The temperature isn't the problem. Amanda is."

"She sure is. This is all her fault," he announces.

Declan's words from earlier ping through me. "Declan said she set this all up. Is that true?"

He nods, then chuckles. "That friend of yours is a determined one, I'll tell you. Marching into my office like that yesterday."

"WHAT?" I motion to the wall of bottles and tap my glass. The mystery shop says to order two drinks, but what the heck—I'll pay for my third.

He gives me a single shot in a glass and upturned eyebrows. "That's it for now."

"Tell me more about Amanda barging into your office!"

"She came to find out the story about Declan and how our mother died." Something in him dials down a bit. The bar's emptying out and I look at the clock. It's early dinnertime, and people are either commuting or getting ready to eat.

"We know how she died," I say with as much sympathy as I can.

"Amanda wanted the whole story."

"Did you give it to her?"

"Yes."

"And....?"

"And told us we needed to go undercover for this mystery shop. To get Declan to see you."

"Huh?"

He runs a frustrated hand through his light-brown hair and looks like a younger version of Declan. It makes me smile. Then again, the television news could show footage of a serial killer and I'd smile. What's in this scotch that makes the world so...good?

"Shannon, I have never seen my brother so happy with any woman before. When he was dating you he was happy. Happy and Declan don't go together. Not since Mom died and Dad blamed Dec for her death."

"Why would he?" I gasp, horrified at the thought. "He was eighteen and a wasp stung her— what did Declan have to do with that?"

The eyes that meet mine are haunted. Just like Declan's.

"Because on that day, I was stung and so was Mom. We only had one EpiPen."

No.

"And we were at one of my soccer games, just goofing around. There were these long trails on the outskirts of the playing field, most of them two or so miles long. Mom loved to walk along the paths and see the creeks, stand on the bridges and listen to the water rush by. She said it was a welcome reprieve from the craziness of business life with Dad."

My own inbreaths feel like icicles entering me

and piercing my heart.

Andrew clears his throat. "The three of us were walking, a good mile away from the soccer fields, when a swarm hit us. Just blasted right over our heads, but a few strays stuck around. Mom was stung twice, I was stung three or four times. We knew about Mom's allergy. She had an EpiPen."

I'm stone cold sober suddenly.

"But we didn't know I was allergic, too, until that moment." His voice has a sing-songy quality to it. He's reciting a well-honed story, one that took telling and retelling to shape.

I can imagine it all in my mind. All too well. Because I just lived it with Declan a very short while ago, in my own way.

"One of my stings was near my eye, another one on my neck, and Mom worked to find her EpiPen for herself, in her giant purse. By the time she found it I was wheezing. Declan started screaming about running back to get help, get an ambulance. I didn't have my phone with me, and I think we later realized neither did Dec, but Mom had one in her purse."

A sick dread fills me.

"And?"

"My wheezing got worse and I remember black spots filled my vision." He shakes his head, hard, like he's trying to force the memory out. "Mom was panicking and shaking, and then she dropped to the ground. Dec came running back and kept shouting. I don't remember the words. Then he grabbed Mom's purse and found her EpiPen."

He gave me a rueful smile. "Mom trained us all—repeatedly—on how to inject her in an emergency."

"Of course," was all I could croak out.

"But when Dec went to her she pushed him away and pointed at me. It felt like I was breathing through a coffee stirrer by then, and the force of blood pumping through me made it sound like—"

"You were under a waterfall," I say, interrupting.

We give each other a knowing look. My words seem to make him stop and close down a bit.

"Can you guess what happened next?" he asks. "Do the math. One EpiPen. One mile from help. One mother's decision."

A painful rush of emotion rolls up the muscles of my throat into the roof of my mouth, through my sinuses, making my eyes water. "Oh, Andrew. Oh, my God. She made Declan inject you, didn't she?"

He closes his eyes and his jaw tightens.

"Yes."

His phone buzzes in his pocket and he grabs it, desperate for a reason to be done with this conversation.

"Gotta go," he says in a clipped voice. Then he pauses, tongue rolling in his cheek, lips parted slightly. His eyes have gone neutral, a skill he shares with his brother.

"So now you know," he adds. "Dad blamed Declan. Said he should have treated Mom."

"But your mother insisted!" Any good mother would. I know my own mom would have done the

167

same, exact thing. Know it with all my heart.

"I know she did. Or," he pauses. "I know she did at least once. I blacked out and woke up in the hospital."

"And your mom..."

"Died the next day. Dec injected me, searched Mom's purse in case there was something he could help her with, found her phone and called for help. Then he ran back to the field. By the time they got to us, it was probably too late for her. But he did everything he could have done. Everything."

"But not enough for James."

Andrew shakes his head slowly. "Never enough for my dad." And with that he purses his lips, breaks eye contact, and steps out into the main lobby, leaving me shivering.

But I'm not cold any more.

Chapter Seventeen

It's 5:17 p.m. now and I decide that maybe I should have a wee bit more than five or six shots of scotch in my stomach as I struggle to comprehend what Andrew's just told me.

Fortunately, part of my job here at The Fort involves eating dinner in the main dining room. Testing whether they'll seat me without reservations happens to be built in to the evaluation, which is great, because not only did I not think ahead to schedule any, my mind is like a series of shrapnel bits spiraling through space after the grenade Andrew just lobbed at me.

A friendly, helpful, extremely insightful grenade, but a dangerous weapon nonetheless. Declan's words from our fight, the day he broke up with me.

I took a chance on you.

Of course, I thought he meant it the same way Steve did—that I was too rough, too jagged-edged, not fit for the upper echelons of society.

Declan meant it in such a different way.

As I approach the restaurant a coiffed, sleek woman who looks like Jessica Coffin's twin, fast-forwarded thirty years, graciously offers me a table. She does not say "for one?" with any condescension, which is important. Business travelers routinely dine alone, and alienating them is not in anyone's financial interest.

I just need a steak and a salad and some equanimity. I think the first two are on the menu. I know the third is not.

I'm seated at a lovely table with a glass waterfall to my right, the water trickling in perfect ribbons onto a Zen rock garden, peaceful and serene. Water lilies—real—float on the pools filled with koi fish, and I inhale deeply, muddling through the thousands of details, snippets of conversation and feelings, that fill me now.

A white-jacketed waiter brings me water and says,

"Enjoying your stay, Ms. Jacoby?"

I flinch and startle, flinging my arms wide, hitting the wine goblet he holds out to me, sending a spray of water all over his very familiar, lined face.

James McCormick.

"What kind of joke is this!" I sputter.

"That was supposed to be my line, Shannon," he mutters as he uses the napkin on his arm to wipe his face.

Whether it's the scotch or the mind blowing story Andrew's just told me, or the aftereffects of just seeing and kissing Declan, I let loose without thinking.

"How could you blame Declan for your wife's death?"

"You don't mince words, do you? I dated a woman like that once. It didn't work out."

"I know. Because she dumped you."

170

His eyes turn into wrinkled triangles. "What are you talking about?"

"The name Winky mean anything to you?" Andrew opened the floodgates with the truth. Well, technically, Amanda did. My head hurts. Too much to tease through, so instead I'll just bulldoze James.

He deserves it.

Reflexively, he looks down at his crotch. Is this a male thing? "Winky? Like that children's television character?"

"Winky the dog."

He sits down next to me, moving just slow enough in that way people in their fifties—even the really fit ones, like my mom—have.

"What kind of joke is this?" He's studying me carefully.

A little too much scotch, way too many revelations, and a flying vibrator that stops traffic have made my day one big, giant crater. "The name Marie Scarlotta mean anything to you?" Mom's maiden name.

James' eyes widen and he searches my face avidly. "My God! I knew you looked familiar." He laughs through his nose. "You're Marie's daughter? And Jacoby is your last name?" He leaps up and disappears around a corner, headed for the kitchen.

That was remarkably anticlimactic.

A worker brings a breadbasket with artisanal options that carry a layer of seeds and nuts on top thicker than an energy bar. James returns, carrying two tumblers of scotch.

Neat.

171

He holds one out to me and with a shaking hand I take it. Seems like the best idea ever, especially right now.

"A toast."

"To extraordinary fathers," I say.

He beams. "Why thank you."

"I was talking about mine."

His smile fades, but he shrugs. "To Jason."

Our glasses crash together, retreat, and then we empty them.

"*He* never accused me of killing someone," I say viciously.

"Is that the baseline for being a good enough parent?" James fingers the rim of his glass. "If so, I've failed." Standing, he pulls off the white jacket and rips off his bow tie. Fit and trim, like Declan, his stomach is flat, shirt a bit askance after his partial undressing. Shrewd eyes meet mine as he raises one hand and a waiter attends to us instantly.

I cover my glass with my hand and shake my head 'no.'

James smiles, baring teeth. He's just wolfish enough to scare me. Not in a sexual predator kind of way.

Just a plain old predator. He's dangerous. Any man who would blame his own son for—

"I regret it. I never should have said that to Declan, and even now, ten years later, I find I can't help myself. It slips out. I'm really angry at me. Not him."

The confession feels insincere.

"You don't believe that." I pull a piece of bread

bigger than my head from the basket and take a bite. The crust is so hard you could use it to stone rape victims in backwards countries with misogynistic laws. I think I just cracked a tooth. Good thing I have whisky to help with the pain.

"What do I believe, Shannon?"

"You're pissed at your wife."

"Because she chose to save Andrew? What kind of a father would feel that? I'm not a monster."

"No, not because of that. Because she died. Period. You're just pissed. Anyone would be. It's human. You're allowed to be human."

He sighs slowly and looks angry.

"And so is Declan," I add.

"If I'd been there, I might have—"

"What? Been racked with guilt like Declan?" I shake my head. "It's a freak accident. They happen. In fact, if Declan hadn't done exactly what his mom told him to do, you might have lost Andrew, too."

"I know."

"And you told Declan to stop dating me because I'm too similar to his mother," I mutter, making the connection.

The booming laugh that greets my statement rattles my teeth. "You? Similar to Elena? No."

"But we have the same affliction."

"Yes."

James worries the glass in front of him and glances at the ice bar, where Andrew's back in place, this time in a suit and tie, talking with what looks like a manager.

"Do you have any idea what it's like to have a

173

child or a wife or a loved one with a severe, anaphylactic allergy like this, Shannon?"

I point to my heart. "Ummm...."

"No." He sighs. "I am absolutely not trivializing what you live with, day in and day out, but no. It's not the same as loving someone who has it."

I frown. Where's he going with this?

"When we learned Elena was severely allergic we went to the best specialists. Took all the preventive measures. Trained the boys and had them tested. I took every damn precaution known to man, mitigated risk as much as possible, and—" He spreads his hands out in a gesture of supplication. "Look what happened."

"You can't live in a bubble," I say, helpless.

"Do you understand," he says through gritted teeth, "what it is like to live in constant, vigilant fear that the person you love can, through the simple, random accident of brushing up against a bee or a wasp, be taken from you? To twitch every spring and to sigh with relief every fall at the first frost? To live in that state incurs a kind of madness."

I really don't know what to say, so I finish my drink and eat more bread.

"Trust me," he says, his eyes searching for and finding Andrew, who is polishing glasses at the bar. James returns his attention to me, his eyes red-rimmed, the loose skin of an old man making him seem even sadder. "That's no way to live your life."

"Neither is cutting off your nose to spite your

174

face."

Resentful eyes meet mine. "Ah, if only life were so simple."

I stand, my appetite long gone, legs wobbly but mind very, very clear. "You make it more complex than it needs to be, and you are teaching your sons all the wrong things. What about love? You loved your wife, didn't you?"

He leaps to his feet. We're making a scene. So much for professional standards. At this point, the ruse that I'm mystery shopping anything other than my own freaking life is over.

"Of course I loved her. More than life itself."

"People say that, but it's not true."

He just stares at me, red-faced and angry.

"If you love anything more than life itself, that means you'd rather be dead. And you're not. You chose to live after her passing."

"That wasn't an easy decision."

"And now you are emotionally crippling your sons!"

"I don't need you to play armchair psychologist with me, Shannon," he spits out.

"You need someone to play psychologist, Dad," says Guido, who has mysteriously appeared behind us. One look at his face, then James' angry eyes, and it all clicks.

"Terrance," I whisper. "You're not Guido."

He gives a twisted smile. "And you're not an executive here for a night."

"What is this?" I demand. "Why are you both and Andrew and Declan all pretending to be hotel employees?"

"Amanda told us—" James starts.

"Really? This was set up by Amanda?"

"She suggested we each take two hours to learn more about the inner life of our property."

"And have you?"

"I've learned quite a bit, Shannon," James says over his shoulder as he leaves. "More than I ever wanted to know."

I take a few shaky steps and stumble. Terrance/Guido grabs my elbow.

"How many drinks did you have?" he asks in that deep voice. My panties are wet, though that might be from the melting bar stools from before.

"Enough to tell your father off."

"That many? I'm impressed." He helps me walk toward the elevator and asks for my floor number. I type in 14 and step back.

"Terrance," I say simply.

"Call me Terry. Impressive," he says, his eyes combing over me.

"You're going to hit on me, too? I'm kind of done with that, thanks," I sigh. Between Declan's kiss and Pete's thigh comments I think I'll become a nun.

"No, just...Declan's spoken so highly of you. Plus you have a really interesting vibrator. I've never seen one before that can fly and stop traffic like that." Those words come out of his mouth just as an older couple comes to the bank of elevators and starts to press the buttons for their floor. The man halts in mid air, finger an inch from the

176

numbers.

Mercifully, my elevator arrives and Terry escorts me on to it. The older couple doesn't join us. We ride in quiet, the enclosed space spinning just a bit, my body warming up to him. Of Declan's brothers he looks the most like him, and for as angry as I am at Declan, I want him, too.

Terry gets me to my room and says, "Nice meeting you, finally."

I snort. "Not that it matters. Declan dumped me. But nice meeting you, Guido."

And with that, I key into my room, flop down on the bed and everything fades to black.

I took a chance on you.

* * *

Someone is knocking on my door. I sit up, disoriented. The wind's blowing the curtains and moonlight streams into the dark room.

Darkness. Nighttime. When did that happen? I climbed onto the bed in the day time, and now...

A glance at the bedside clock tells me it's 10:22 p.m.

What?

I sit up as the person outside the door knocks again, harder this time, like a man banging with the edge of his fist.

"Room service," says a muffled man's voice.

Room service? Did I order room service? I know I was supposed to as part of the mystery shop, but I don't remember it.

I sit up, my mouth dry, and rub my eyes repeatedly. A deep inhale and I launch myself up. A gurgle, deep inside my belly, makes me realize I'm ravenous.

Maybe I did call and order dinner? If so, what the heck am I about to eat?

I open the door and there's Declan, standing behind a room service cart loaded with covered dishes.

I close the door in his face.

Not *that* hungry.

Back pressed against the door, I fight my way to full wakefulness, heart slamming against my breastbone. I'm still mad at him, aren't I? By all rights I should be. And yet as the details from my conversations earlier in the night come flooding in, a calm sense of equivocation fills me. I bite my lower lip, hard, trying to wake up. To shake some sense into me.

Tap tap tap.

"Shannon?" His voice is contrite. This is new. "Please? You need to eat. Andrew and Terry are worried about you."

Worried?

"They said you were drinking quite a bit, something about a guy hitting on you in the bar, my dad being an asshole and..." His voice winds down into a frustrated snarl. "Just let me in. Take the food. I want to make sure you're well."

"What's on the tray?" I ask through the door.

"Filet mignon. Mashed potatoes in a reduced

178

fig and balsamic vinegar sauce. Mocha caramel cheesecake."

I moan. Can't help it.

"No white wine, though. Andrew insisted." There's a big question in his voice. I rub my cheek against the door and take a deep breath, deciding.

Cheesecake wins.

The click of the door sounds like a choice, and I open it, stepping back. Declan rolls the car in and gives me a half smile as he sets the car next to the desk and unloads the trays onto the bed.

"Eat."

"You don't have to worry about me, you know," I insist, but as he pulls the top of the first tray up the scent of steak and spices makes my stomach scream the opposite of my words.

He laughs.

"Just eat."

After he sets the cover down he steps back and looks me up and down. "Nice nap?"

"No. I kept dreaming about a killer bee coming to get me in Antarctica. And a ferocious wolf."

"What a mystery," he deadpans. "No need to guess what your subconscious is struggling to get out."

"What do you dream about, Declan?" I pick up a fresh strawberry from a fruit plate and eat it, grateful for something to fill my mouth after asking.

"You."

"Nice," I say, tipping my chin up, hurrying to swallow. "Really. Great line."

"It's not a line." I take a bite of potato and then

another, suddenly starving. Declan pulls the desk chair away from the keyboard tray and turns it backwards, straddling it.

Oh. So he's staying. And we're talking.

So that's how it is.

I cut into the steak and take a bite. It's like eating butter, just right, the perfect cut of tenderloin. "Tell me more about your dreams," I insist as I eat, then I stop. "Would you like some?"

"I already ate." His voice is raw. "I enjoy watching you."

"Dreams," I demand. "Dreams."

Chapter Eighteen

"When I dream about you, it's all sweetness and light. I don't remember the dreams," he confesses. "Not the way normal people do. I see pictures. Still images. Flashes."

"Not like a movie reel? That's how my dreams work. The parts I remember," I explain. The filet is the size of a silver dollar and I finish it in five bites, then move on to the potatoes, then some julienned vegetables. Our conversation is so...normal. Concrete.

Cradling his jaw in his palm, he leans his propped elbow against the back of the leather chair. "No. Even as a kid. I compared notes with Terry once and he ribbed me about it. Said I was weird for not having dreams like him and Andrew." Declan shrugs, eyes a little too bright, throat tight. I pause my dinner and take a long, slow drink of water, enjoying the moment to look at him.

He's nervous.

Nervous.

My soul starts to hope.

I unveil a piece of mocha caramel cheesecake that could feed a small village in Southeast Asia. Grabbing two forks, I hold one out to him like an olive branch.

"Have some with me."

"I'm not hungry."

"Look at that! It's a work of art. If you don't want a single bite of it, then you're not human," I joke.

We simultaneously take a bite and groan together. Mutual mouthgasms. They're rare, but when they happen, they're unbelievable.

He gets to the cheesecake before me for a second bite.

"I thought you weren't hungry," I tease.

"God, I've missed you," he says, vulnerable and watching me like I'm the only woman he's ever seen. I swallow and stop, fork jabbed into the dessert, hanging in suspension. My shaking hand reaches for the water goblet and I finish it, Declan's breath tortured, the air in the room singed with anticipation.

"If you missed me," I say in a hoarse voice that seems to come from a place nine inches away from my mouth, "why haven't you called? Or texted? Or sent a bat signal?"

"Remember that whole idiot thing from earlier today? Yeah. That."

"And then there's your mom."

This time, he doesn't flinch. Just closes his eyes and sighs, then opens them, fighting for composure. I want to reach out, to touch him, to connect my skin to his but he has to make the first move. Simply knowing what happened ten years ago and making the connection doesn't mean he's here to reunite.

He has to be the one to say it.

Leaping to his feet, he begins to pace. There's a nervous tension in him, like an animal that has been caged for so long it doesn't know what to do when freed. Three times he traverses the small room, words pouring out.

"You know my mother died from that damn wasp sting. Andrew was stung. First time he had a full-blown anaphylaxis." The medical term comes out in a robotic voice, but as he continues he becomes more emotional. "Mom kept pointing from the EpiPen to him. She fought me off when I tried to jab it in her leg. Fought me. She couldn't speak by then. The words came out as grunts. Andrew was panicking and they were both dying."

"I know." I walk to him and stop him, reaching for both his hands. "I know."

"That day when you were stung," he says, eyes wild, pulse beating so hard I can see it in his neck, right under his earlobe. "When you were stung and your EpiPen came out my first thought was Thank God, only one person. Only one person who I am responsible for. The odds aren't stacked against me."

"And then I stabbed you," I say with a choked, horrified snort, squeezing his warm hands.

"And I thought that was it. But you had a second one." He doesn't need to say what we're both thinking. The room goes cold with a huge gust from a brewing storm on the bay. If only...

"Fate," I blurt out.

"Fate," he says without question. "Fate is a cruel mistress."

I look at him with a questioning face.

"Of all the women I could have met with their hand down a toilet at one of my stores, it had to be the one with the same allergy that...."

"Yeah. It's pretty freaking weird."

"I shouldn't be with you."

I freeze.

"But I can't do this."

Do what?

"I can't stay away. Dad tried to convince me that I'm signing up for nothing but heartbreak with you. That the genetics are stacked against us—"

Genetics?

"That our children have a higher chance of—"

CHILDREN? Did he just say *children*?

"And I'll spend the rest of my life in fear of—"

In a mad rush I tackle him, the kiss desperate and urgent, my body launching into his with such force that we fall onto the bed, a mass of pillows rolling off and bouncing, pelting our legs as his mouth meets mine, rougher with each second, claiming me.

"I can't be without you," he says in a hurried gasp. "I've tried. You're forthright and honest and the most upfront woman I've ever met. You have an inner core that makes you turn toward the good. You make me want to be good, too." He kisses the end of my nose and pulls back, half in shadows and half in moonlight. The room is timeless, his face pensive. Thoughtful.

"And you have a very weird family."

"And a malicious cat," I add, peppering his jaw

184

with kisses.

"You don't give a damn what people think, at the same time you care about what people feel. And you took on my dad." I can feel his grin through our kiss. "That's when I fell in love with you."

"The same day you *dumped* me you fell in love with me?"

"Love isn't rational."

I fell in love with you.

"When you said you took a chance on me, that was..."

"My being an idiot. Not the taking a chance part." He pulls my shirt out from the waistline of my skirt and rests his palms against my back. The feeling charges me, making my skin hum. "The jumbled mess of thinking that I should just walk away. That the pain of being with you outweighed the joy."

Joy.

"And you're here because..."

"Because I couldn't stay away."

"You had to pretend to be Alfredo the Plumber in order to tell me this?"

"Did it work?"

"I don't know. You'll have to ask me again. At breakfast." The smoldering look he gives me as he pulls me to him in a kiss makes my toes tingle. Dishes on the tray rattle and he sits up, moves the tray, and stands in the moonlight, the lines of his clothed body like a work of art.

I stand pressing in for a kiss, and begin to unbutton his shirt. "Forthright, huh?" One knowing touch as I reach down makes him suck air in through his teeth.

"I like a woman who knows what she wants."

"Then you must *really* like me, because I know exactly what—and who—I want."

My own breath is foreign to me, the spellbinding touch of his fingers on my cheek like a caress from a different world. He's different now, deeper and richer in his intents, and I want to believe him. Need to believe him. My body responds before my heart, so quick to react that I pause, listening to the beat of blood pounding through me, all rushing to the surface of my skin to get closer to him.

I hold nothing back now and invite him to cast aside whatever keeps him from surrendering to the new reality we've woven just by being together, right here. Right now. I don't need to hear him tell me he loves me—it's too soon for that—but I need him to show me.

Show me.

His hands take in my skin like a man in charge, grasping what he wants, possessing it. As I reach for his pants and unsnap them, his fingers make quick work of undoing my bra, then his heat is on me, warm palms cupping my breasts, the pleasure of being together and intimate nakedly on display in the look he gives me, open and revealing.

Trust. He trusts me, now, and joy pours through my body like liquid fire, my lips quivering from emotion, my whole being at rest and yet in eager motion. He slips my shirt, then bra, off my shoulders and onto the floor as he steps out of his clothes. We're both naked and raw before one another in the blink of an eye, and we both feel it. The shockwave of peace and hope, of arousal and yearning.

Of coming home.

"This is what you want," he murmurs against my shoulder as he seeds it with tiny kisses, repeating my own words back.

"Yes."

"Me, too. More than anything. This is...everything. You are everything."

"Then let's be everything together."

"High standards."

"I know you're an overachiever."

His deep, throaty chuckle morphs into something more sensual as he gently guides me to the bed, the full length of him covering me. All my jokes disintegrate, replaced by a moment-by-moment awareness that makes me feel ancient, alive and immortal, regenerated kiss by kiss, stroke by stroke, lick by—

"Oh, there," I whisper, the sound half groan, half sigh, as he makes me speechless once more. We're just kissing, but it's so much more, his mouth sensual and alive, our hands roaming and remembering, searching and loving. Each lush kiss makes me go to a level inside myself that I didn't know I possess, and Declan's right there with me, a fiery, passionate presence.

"You know," he says as my hands ride up from the grooves of his hipbones, over his sharp belly, abs like inverted shells under perfect, musky skin, "this isn't part of your evaluation."

I laugh as he kisses the base of my throat, my fingertips memorizing him, reaching down to feel his tight ass. "How do you know? Maybe this is in my app."

"Do you find the lovemaking aesthetically pleasing?" he says, his hands making damn certain that I do.

"I need more time and observation to make that kind of determination," I say in a faux-prim voice.

The teasing fades as he kisses me again, then dips his head down to tongue one tight rosebud nipple. Again? This is new. Then again, we've never had all the time in the world, our own hotel room, and a bed the size of my backyard.

"As you wish," he adds, showing me exactly how to perform exemplary customer service, the rough rasp of the soft hair on his thighs and calves tickling my hips. We're a slow, languid twinning of warmth now, and Declan stops to look at me.

Really look at me.

No modestly, no walls to hide emotion behind. We watch each other for longer than is decent, the air telescoping to a pinpoint, his eyes a cavern of delight. He's inviting me to join him with this look, and I intertwine my fingers in his, shift my thigh just so to stroke him, the resulting gasp the only answer either of us needs to give.

The moonlight spilling into the room gives me all the visual access I could wish to revel in, my eyes feasting on the sharp lines of his body, how muscle dominates in all the empty spaces between bones. Fluid and graceful, Declan moves like a man who knows himself, and I adopt the same, even as it is not in my nature.

Who says it's not?

His kisses travel lower, attending to my breasts, then down the valley and into the fertile lands where his mouth makes me arch up in surprise and pleasure. He takes his time, hands under me, generous with his effort, erotic with his skill. My hands find his shoulder blades, admiring the fine, artistic lines of his muscled back, then stroke up the nape of his neck to bury in his hair. He is at my essence, tasting all I have to offer, and he is giving in bold, breathtaking ways.

My release is so close, a glow that fills me from top to bottom, and I reach down, curl up, and pull his mouth to mine, wanting more intimacy, wanting him face-to-face. His lips are tangy and savory, his smile all mine, and I nudge him to lie down on the bed, pulling myself up onto my knees.

In full glory, oh—I can't quite catch my breath, the handsome, powerful pull of his skin and blood next to me magnetic. I want him to belong to me. I want to be claimed.

I want.

I want.

Declan tugs gently on my knee and guides me to straddle him. He turns to take care of practicalities, a condom on him quickly, and I am on him, not leaning forward with rounded shoulders and self-conscious posture, but riding high, sitting straight up, breasts gleaming in the shadow of the city lights and the moon's eye.

"You are..." He finishes the sentence with a sighing sound more gratifying than any word. Eyes the color of Irish hills gaze at me with an intensity that brands me. I am his. He is mine.

I don't need to hear the word love. Not yet. Because I know that someday I will. The certainty inside me is so solid, so secure that as he fills me, our connection complete, I will the words to span between us without being spoken. Appreciative, smoking eyes take me in as he pushes up, touching my core, we are one. One flesh, one heart. I feel it beating, strong and pattering under my hand, pulse pounding as we rock to ecstasy.

This is how we find each other.

We tremor together on a frequency of our own creation, and then, with dawning awareness, find the divine within.

Chapter Nineteen

"You have such nice hands." In the morning light, his big hands look like an artist carved them, the thick veins and muscled thumb pad like an artifact you would find in a display case in a Greek museum. I'm pressed against him under the covers, a handful of pillows under our shoulders and heads, and we're luxuriating in the sheer quantity of skin that can touch each other when we're naked, in a bed, and alone.

The way life should be.

He inhales slowly and stretches like a big lion, the thick triceps in his arms bulging and thinning out, making a deep groove in his arm as the muscles pull away from each other. Does the man have any fat on him? I have plenty for us both, I suppose. As if reading my mind he reaches for my ass and gives it a love pat.

My phone buzzes.

"Ignore it," he groans, breathing with a slight sound of deep satisfaction. "I don't want to deal with people just yet."

"What about me?" I pretend to pout.

"You're not people."

"What am I, then?"

"You're prey." With a playful roar he pins me beneath him, demonstrating that all of his body isn't nearly as sleepy as he's pretending to be. Some parts woke up a bit earlier and are standing at attention, ready to, er....plunge into the day.

Bzzzzz.

And then my hotel phone rings.

We look at each other in alarm. "I have to answer that," I say with a pleading tone.

"Of course." He lets me go and I grab the receiver.

"Hello?"

"Shannon?" It's Amanda.

"Who is it?" Declan asks just loud enough for her next words to be:

"YOU HAVE A MAN IN YOUR ROOM WITH YOU?" She screams so loudly I fling the receiver across the bed and hold my palm over my ear, moaning in pain. Declan winces and sits up, scrambling for the phone, which slides off the bed like a paralyzed snake with no ability to save itself from plummeting.

"Amanda? It's Declan. Shannon will be back in a second. She's just sewing her eardrum back together."

The ringing in my ear isn't fading, and Declan gives me an awkward look. I'm completely naked and his eyes drift down.

Now he looks like a wolf.

"Fine, and you?" he says, making strange small talk with the woman who mysteriously set last night's events into motion. I have a million words for her, most of them involving some combination of "thank" and "you," but right now I'm staring,

192

agog, at my naked—boyfriend?—talking about the weather with Amanda.

I snatch the phone back and wave him off to the bathroom. As he stands, his ass muscles make me whimper.

"Ear hurts that bad?' she asks softly.

I wipe a line of drool from my mouth as I get a very nice view of Declan making coffee in the Keurig. "Um, yes. It's torture. Why are you calling me in my room? You can't do that. It could break my cover. Plus, what the hell did you do? Andrew told me you barged into his office and demanded to know about Declan and his mother's death, and then I came here to do this mystery shop and it's a plague of McCormicks! Terry and Andrew and Declan and James all pretended to work here."

Silence.

"Amanda?"

"Um." Her tone of voice is hesitant. If she were calling because someone got hurt, she'd say so. This is business, and a cold dread fills me.

"What's going on? Tell me why you set all this up."

"That's not why I'm calling."

"Then why?"

"Greg's been trying to call you. Me, too. Shannon, go get your smartphone and log in to your Twitter account."

"Say what? I don't need to read any more crap from Jessica Coffin right now." I give Declan a once-over as he makes the second mug of coffee. "Especially right now."

"Yeah, well, it's about your mom. And Jessica. And the credit union client."

"What do those three completely unrelated things have to do with each other?"

"Marie made them not-so unrelated last night."

"Speak in English, please."

"Well, she, uh..."

"Spit it out!"

"Your mom started taunting Jessica Coffin on Twitter and insisting that you were pretending to be a lesbian for the credit union shop, and Jessica looped the client in, and now they're insisting Greg fire you."

I asked for the full story and got it. In one sentence.

"Say that again," I peep. Declan's frowning now and he hands me the hot cup of coffee, a concerned look on his face.

She takes a deep breath and repeats it, word for word.

"I'm *fired*?"

Declan's eyebrows shoot up and he mouths the word. I shrug. None of this makes sense.

"Not yet, but when Greg calls..."

"Was this because I didn't do the mystery shop I'm on right now correctly?" The words come out of my mouth and I know they're wrong, but what she's saying doesn't make sense.

"No, honey. It's because your mom and Jessica publicly blew your cover and the client basically needs to save face. It's all public relations. They need a fall guy. And that's...you."

"*I'm* the fall guy?"

She sighs. "Yes. I'm so sorry," she adds in a rush. "Greg feels awful about it and argued with the client forever, but they are absolutely adamant. The credit union called the client and it's turned into a nasty mess."

"Have you talked to my mom?"

Amanda pauses mid breath. "She, uh, didn't really understand what a see-you-next-Tuesday Jessica could be."

My jaw drops. "She didn't realize that? After everything we've dealt with?"

"I think your mom just turned into a Mama Bear and went crazy."

"Like that's different from...what?" Declan crawls on the bed and starts massaging my shoulders, which are two big lumps of granite right now. Fired. I'm fired.

Fired for doing my job.

Fired for nearly losing the man who is right behind me, touching me with tenderness and compassion, trying to massage the crazy away.

Fired for being loved by a mother who has the business skills of a sno-cone salesman in a blizzard.

Bzzzzz. I haven't even reached for my phone to look at the Twittermess. I can only imagine. But Declan reaches across me, smelling like sex and spice and mmmmm, and hands me my phone.

Greg.

"Is that Greg on your phone?" Amanda asks with a pitying voice.

"This is real. You're serious," I whisper.

"I wish I weren't. Trust me."

Declan peels the receiver from my fingers carefully. "Answer the phone, Shannon. Get it over with. It's like ripping a Band-Aid off. It's better to just do it." The look he gives me is no-nonsense, but understanding at the same time.

I take a deep breath, hit Talk, and say, "You don't have to say it, Greg. I already know."

Declan heads to the bathroom to give me some privacy. I hear the shower turn on as Greg blusters and apologizes, rants and overexplains. His words pour over me as I wonder how my life could pivot like this in less than twenty-four hours.

I get my (ex) boss off the phone quickly so I can go shower with my (ex-ex) boyfriend. Just as I knock on the door the water stops. Great. He's one of those people who can take a three-minute shower.

Freak.

"Come in." I open the door a crack and poke my head in. He's toweling off. His face softens into a look of compassion.

"You okay?"

"I'm fired."

"Come here." He opens his arms and I walk into his embrace, still in a state of shock. Even my libido is stunned, because the press of his clean, wet wall of skin against my body isn't making me hump his leg.

"I have more student loan debt than you could ever imagine. Plus credit cards, and now I won't have a car because I have to give the Turdmobile

196

back. And as bad as it was driving that piece of—"

"Shhhhhh," he urges. "It'll be fine."

"Fine? No, it won't! You try finding a good, steady job in this economy. I have a marketing degree. I'm lucky I haven't spent the last year handing out new product samples at Costco for $15 an hour!"

"You'll find a better job," he says with confidence.

For some reason, his reassurance is annoying. "I hope you're right."

"I know I am." He rests his chin on my head. "Because I want you to come work for me."

My laughter makes my breasts bounce against his chest. "Ha ha."

He pulls away, eyes dead serious. "I mean it. Come work at Anterdec. Assistant Director of Marketing."

"I really don't need you to make fun of me right now."

"I don't joke about business. We'll pay you more, Anterdec has great benefits, and you'll get stock options, bonus, and a great maternity leave package." He winks.

"I can't believe you're saying this." I feel numb.

"Did I overdo it on the maternity comment?" He makes a sheepish face. "Didn't mean to over play my hand."

"No, I mean that you'd think I'd just jump right in and take a job working for you, that you'd ride in on your white horse and rescue me."

"That's not what I—"

I start to shake. Can't control it, can't mute it. Just...shake. It's all too much, from Guido being Terry to my confrontation with James to reuniting with Declan and now I'm fired?

And Declan wants to wrap me up in gauze and make me his little porcelain doll.

Nope.

"I, um, need a shower. Don't you have a business meeting or something you need to get to?" I mutter as I turn on the water and climb in. I couldn't hint any more if I shoved him out the door and threw his clothes at him.

Declan's face appears between the tiled wall and the shower curtain, like Jack Nicholson breaking through the door in the old version of The Shining. Okay, not quite that bad, but...

"You're not getting rid of me that easily," he says, and climbs on in with me.

"You just showered!" I protest. The slick feel of his skin against mine as he holds me from behind is at odds with my righteous indignation, which I'm holding onto by a thin thread.

"I can get wet again." He turns me around, the hot spray glorious against my back, my hair hanging in limp strands against my cheekbones and shoulders, Declan's second head definitely not limp. "And my eyes are up here," he coaxes.

I raise mine. "Oops."

"You're ogling me."

"Yes."

"Good." He kisses me so deeply I think my

198

toes have curled into themselves. "Don't be mad. I really mean it about the job. I thought about offering it to you a while ago."

"How long ago?"

"The day you showed up at that meeting after the toilet incident."

"That long ago?" I eye him with suspicion. "Why?"

"Because you're smart."

"Pffft. That's not a good enough reason! No one gets a great job with a huge megacorporation because they're *smart*," I say, making a dismissive sound with the back of my throat.

"Then how do you get a great job with a megacorporation?" he asks.

"By knowing someone—" I groan. "Networking."

His hands squeeze my ample ass. "Is that what they call this?" He kisses the hollow at the nape of my neck. "Networking?"

"You can't give me a job just because you're sleeping with me! What kind of feminist would I be if I did that?"

"An *employed* feminist?"

I stop and consider that for a moment as his hand does unspeakable things. Really. He's making it hard for me to speak. "Would I work under you?"

He makes a suggestive sound.

"How about we conduct a little employee orientation right now?" he whispers.

And then he schools me.

Chapter Twenty

"Check out that headline," Josh crows as he slaps a morning paper on my desk at work. Um, former work, technically. I'm here to clean out my desk.

Unidentified Flying Orgasm screams the newspaper headline, with a giant picture of a crushed vibrator on the ground next to the bumper of a taxi, two men arguing over it.

"Nice."

"Funny how that happened at the exact hotel where you were working," he adds with a sly look.

"The world is made up of unremitting coincidences."

"And you have an awful lot of them following you around." He walks out of my office and into his. Keyboard keys click furiously in the distance.

I make a dismissive sound in my throat and continue putting my personal stuff in a box. Greg isn't here today, but he's called me three times in the past two days to apologize profusely. I get a month's severance and can continue to mystery shop for him, but he can't chance losing the second-biggest client for Consolidated Evalu-shop.

I get it. I really do understand. And there's a silver lining. A big one.

Carol's taking my job. She screamed in my ear

after Greg interviewed her, and Mom and Dad can fill in for child care during the occasional non-school hours she has to work. It's a relief to know that even as my own career turns to shambles, at least my sister and nephews are in a better place.

"Hey," Josh whispers, carrying his laptop with him. I'm about to hand mine over and he'll back up all my personal files, then wipe it clean for Carol. "I need to show you something."

He clicks on a tab with Twitter open. On Jessica Coffin's profile. I groan.

"No, no, just look," he assures me. His eyes are lit up and he's so animated, which means I'm about to learn all about Linux sftp protocol scripting or he'll explain some intricate detail about how the darknet will take over the world when the Millennial Illuminati gain power.

"I really have no desire to even think about Jessica Coffin again."

"She's getting completely trashed online. Twitter, Facebook, Pinterest, Tumbler—you name it. There's a long, long thread on Reddit calling her out."

Now I'm interested. "What happened?"

He waves his hands in front of him with glee, face consumed by the glowing screen. "Someone," he says in an arched tone, "appears to have hacked into her Twitter account and is posting all of the direct, private messages she's been receiving for the past year."

"Huh?"

"Basically, people have been feeding her

202

gossip and now they're all being outed by her. Her Twitter stream, that is."

"Why would she do that?"

"She's not doing it. A cracker did it."

"A cracker?"

His harsh sigh makes me feel stupid. "A hacker."

"So do I know this 'someone'?"

Pride shines through in his upright posture and he strokes his chin. "I can't imagine knowing anyone who would do such a thing, but you never know. Could be 4chan, or..." He goes on and names a bunch of groups I've never heard of.

I stare at the screen and read some of the messages.

Many are from Steve. Busted!

A wide smile stretches my face as I turn my own computer off and hand it to Josh. "Thanks."

"For what?" He looks at the ceiling and pretends to be innocent.

I stand on tiptoes and kiss his cheek. "For helping to balance the world a little more fairly." My keychain rattles in my hand as I palm it off on him.

"Company car?"

"Yep. You can take the Turdmobile and hand your car off to my sister when she starts working here. Though my nephew, Jeffrey, would be disappointed. He wants to drive around in a 'pieth of thit car'."

Josh laughs, then swallows, hard. "I'm going to miss you."

"I'm not disappearing."

"But you won't be here. You and Amanda are this amazing duo. Someone has to huddle with me in the winter to stay warm."

"Carol's a big girl like me. You'll do fine."

We hug.

My phone buzzes. It's Declan, outside, in a limo. Josh walks me to the main doors and peers out at my mode of transportation.

"What the hell am I worried about," he declares. "You're leaving this place and the Turdmobile to get into that?" A low whistle and a high five ends my visit, and I turn to Declan with my personal belongings in a box, walking away from the very job that made me meet him.

Car tires screech in the parking lot as Amanda arrives. She parks across two spaces and jumps out, running to me. Josh stands in the doorway, gawking.

"Wait! Stop!" Breathless, she leans over and puts her hands on her knees. Declan climbs out of the limo and takes the box from me, a curious look passing between us.

"Mystery shopping emergency? Did someone fail to deliver a drive-thru order in ninety seconds or less?" I joke.

"No." She's in tears. "I just didn't want to miss you before you left."

"You could just text me," I say slowly, trying to keep the joke going because if I don't, I'll dissolve into a puddle of tears, too. "You didn't need to pull a Hollywood moment where you rush in and—"

Too late. We're sobbing. Two strong, masculine arms wrap around me and Amanda and then we hear the whimpering sound of Josh crying, too.

"It's not going to be the same," he wails.

Declan unbuttons his suit jacket, crosses his arms, and leans back against the limo. His eyes roll skyward. "It'll be a few minutes, Gerald," he says to the driver through the open window.

"That's right!" Amanda squeaks, flashing indignant eyes at my boyfriend. "You get her for the rest of her life. We only have her for a few more minutes."

"We're all going to that tapas bar in Waltham at 7 p.m. tonight, remember?" Declan answers dryly. "If you can suffer through five hours of not seeing Shannon."

"That's not the point!" Josh gasps, wiping his eyes. "It's just the end of an era. You don't get it."

Declan nods slowly. "You're right. I don't." He gives me a warm grin and cocks an eyebrow like he's saying *WTF is up with your friends?*

"He's right," I say to Amanda and Josh, laughing through tears. "It's not like you'll never see me again. We'll have chevre-stuffed pimentoes in a few hours."

The three of us compose ourselves, give final hugs, and they walk into the building while I climb into the limo with Declan, where he's sitting, waiting for me.

Arms outstretched and tissues at the ready.

The drive over to Anterdec involves a lot of hitched sobbing and, fortunately, no eyerolling.

"I'm fine! And no, I haven't officially decided." For the past week Declan's been pestering me to just say yes and come work for him.

And for the past week I've dug my heels in and told him I hadn't made a decision.

My terms: a meeting with James to make sure I can tolerate working here.

In Declan's mind this is a done deal.

In my mind it's an open case. Nothing is settled. Putting all of my emotional and financial life in the hands of one man is a risk that involves an extraordinary amount of trust, and while we're back together and it's clear—so clear—that we're meant for each other, I'm a pragmatist at heart.

A little OCD, even. Which is great when it comes to managing 34,985 details for marketing campaigns, but not so great when it comes to taking flying leaps of faith and love.

Working for Declan means working for James, and I didn't exactly leave off on a good note the last time I saw him.

I'm fairly cleaned up and halfway decent by the time the limo pulls in to the Anterdec private garage. Unlike the main entrance, this is a quiet, subterranean section of the parking labyrinth that I would never know existed if it weren't for Declan.

I say so.

He looks at me, eyebrows crowded, and shrugs. "Isn't that the point?"

I laugh, the sound like ping pong balls being

dropped on a trampoline. "You really have no idea how real people live."

"Your mom is taking me thrifting, remember? I'll be sure to have Jeeves scuff my shoes just so and to forget to shave." His pretend British accent and locked jaw make me laugh harder. Sweat covers my palms, my makeup's long been cried off or kissed off (I much prefer the latter), and I wonder just how raw I must appear.

An audience of James McCormick in this kind of fragile state is really not appealing.

"Mom will make you dumpster dive if you're not careful," I warn him.

Very real horror fills his face. "What?" He looks a bit sick. "I thought that chicken tasted a bit odd when she had us over for dinner last night."

I punch him. We get out of the limo and board the elevator. "Not food. She goes behind florist shops and card stores and comes home with a mountain of stuff to add to the mountain of stuff in the basement."

He pauses and reaches for my shoulders, locking eyes on me. "Are your parents okay financially? Do they need—"

I press my index finger against his lips. "The fastest way to wind up dead and decomposing in a 55-gallon drum in Dad's Man Cave is to offer financial help to my parents."

He gulps. "Understood. But—dumpster diving?"

"It's a hobby. Mom does this. Wait three months and she'll get over it. Last year it was the whole Extreme Couponing thing."

We ride up a few floors in silence and he turns to me with a look of dawning recognition. "Extreme Couponing. Is that why you have what looks like hundreds of deodorants jammed in the drawers of your bathroom."

I wink. "You connected the dots."

"I just thought you were obsessive about not having smelly armpits..."

"She goes crazy on triple coupon day. You should see her stash of sex lube."

With that the elevator doors open.

And there stands James McCormick, who clearly heard my and Declan's last words.

"Make her take the job, Dad," Declan announces, face impassive as he leans over and kisses my cheek. My fingers grope for his arm but he's slick and eludes my attempt.

"Not if she has smelly armpits," James jokes. We walk quietly to the private door to his office where he motions toward two enormous wingback chairs pointed toward the windows.

"Please. Sit. Coffee?"

My hands are shaking. Don't need to add a caffeine injection. "No, thank you."

He sits next to me and leans forward, forearms on knees, eyes perceptive. "Declan tells me you are hesitating on taking the Assistant Director of Marketing job."

"Yes."

"Because of me." It's not a question.

Honesty is best here. "Because I don't want to

208

be too dependent on Declan."

One eyebrow slowly rises. "Go on."

"There isn't any more to it." I shrug. "It's that simple. We're together, and I am concerned about mixing business with..." I frown.

"With life." He nods, rubbing his hands together slowly.

"Yes."

"Declan tells me you're good." He clears his throat. "With marketing."

H e *really* didn't need to elaborate. Now I'm self-conscious.

"And he is willing to take a larger risk than you, Shannon. I think you need to take that into consideration." There's a hard edge to his voice, but it's encased in a velvet tongue.

"What?"

"Not in business. But in choosing to love you. To stay with you. To—perhaps—build a life with you."

Love.

"I'm not in a pity relationship," I answer bluntly. "He's not offering me a relationship, or a job, because—"

"That is evident." James McCormick doesn't listen to extraneous words. "My point is that Declan, who has one of the smartest, most rational minds I know, has decided that giving his heart to you is worth the risk that you may not be around to share it."

A cold rush pours through me.

"What does that—"

"While you dither and pretend you don't know whether to take the job, Declan is living his choice every day. He's taken a much bigger risk already than you would take if you accept the job at Anterdec."

I just blink.

"Take the job, Shannon. Worry about what-if later. You can't spend your life worrying that the devil you don't know might turn bad when the devil you do know already is. Unemployment doesn't suit you."

No. it didn't. I've gotten so bored this week that Chuckles now has painted toenails and you can eat off my dad's Man Cave floor.

"Why are you urging me to do it? Take the job?"

"You make Declan happy."

"Nope. Not enough."

"Because you're Marie's daughter and it feels like karma."

"Still not enough."

He sighs. "Because of all the women Declan has dated, you are the first one I've met who is remotely interesting. And challenging. I don't surround myself with yes men and I'd prefer not to be surrounded by yes daughters-in-law."

Daughter in law.

"Therefore, I ask you to take some time to decide, and—"

"Yes."

"Yes?"

"Yes."

210

"That was fast."

"When you know, you know."

James looks over my shoulder and I follow his gaze. He's looking at a picture of his late wife. She's on the beach with all three boys; I'm guessing Declan is about twelve in the photo, braces on his teeth and a layer of baby fat in his face that says the long stretch of puberty hasn't hit yet.

It's a happy photo. A joyous one, even.

"Yes, Shannon. When you know, you know."

Chapter Twenty-One

I spend the next few hours in Human Resources, kept busy on an assembly line of managers and coordinators, never once seeing Declan. The Associate Director for HR gave me my salary proposal, benefits information, and when my eyes bugged out of my head at the salary, she was polite enough not to tell me to shove them back in my head.

We're taught in business classes to negotiate. Always. But when someone offers you more than twice your old salary and a benefits package valued at nearly a year's pay—you just say thank you profusely. I'm sure Steve would argue the opposite, but Steve can go suck a box of rocks.

My phone buzzes in the middle of signing paperwork. Mom. I keep it to text.

You okay? She texts. *Need a chocolate intervention?*

Nope. Signing my new hire paperwork at Anterdec.

The phone rings. "You're coming to my yoga class on Saturday still, right? And bringing Declan."

"You cannot use him to sell more spots in your class, Mom. He's not a side show like a sword swallower or The Bearded Woman."

She makes a tsking sound. "We already have that! And Corrine is trying to get it under control with electrolysis, so stop making jokes about her."

"I wasn't!" The HR coordinator who is explaining my health insurance package comes back with her photocopies. "I have to go."

"Congratulations, honey! What's your salary?" The coordinator takes my empty coffee mug and motions, asking if I want more. I nod yes.

"Shannon?"

I tell Mom my salary.

"You make more than Jason!" she squeals.

"Will he feel emasculated?" I ask, worried.

"*Pffft.* If that man can stay married to me for nearly thirty years, he can handle this. Your father doesn't do emasculation. Well, not in public, anyhow."

"Mom," I growl.

"Fine, fine. I'll make a celebratory dinner tonight! Bring Declan over! We'll play Cards Against Humanity and I'll break out the new candles I found in the dumpster."

"Living it up!"

"I'm so proud of you, Shannon."

"Thanks, Mom."

The HR person comes back in and after two more hours, I have a photo ID, a start date, and a raging case of missing Declan.

Bzzzz.

Meet me where the limo is, he texts.

The receptionist guides me to the right elevator

and I ride it down, completely drained. A happy kind of drain. The kind of exhaustion you feel when your entire paradigm about how to live your life has changed.

The elevator doors open and there's Declan, holding two epipens and a dozen long-stemmed chocolate covered strawberries (a mix of dark and milk, of course) in his arms.

And he's wearing a grin that makes my heart do jumping jacks.

"Do you, Shannon Jacoby, promise to be my Assistant Director of Marketing so long as your stock options may vest?"

"I do."

He kisses me with a freedom and abandon that makes the world disappear.

And I swear, somewhere, my mother is banging a spoon against a wine glass, finger ready to dial Farmington Country Club to reserve a date in 2016.

Someone get Steve's mom some smelling salts. And a dose for him, too.

THE END

Other Books by Julia Kent

Suggested Reading Order

Her First Billionaire—FREE
Her Second Billionaires
Her Two Billionaires
Her Two Billionaires and a Baby
Her Billionaires: Boxed Set

It's Complicated

Complete Abandon (A Her Billionaires novella)
Complete Harmony (A Her Billionaires novella #2)

Random Acts of Crazy
Random Acts of Trust
Random Acts of Fantasy
Random Acts of Hope

"Share Me" in the anthology Spring Fling

Maliciously Obedient
Suspiciously Obedient
Deliciously Obedient (the trilogy is done!)

Shopping for a Billionaire 1
Shopping for a Billionaire 2
Shopping for a Billionaire 3
Shopping for a Billionaire 4

About the Author

Text JKentBooks to 77948 and get a text message on release dates!

New York Times and *USA Today* bestselling author Julia Kent turned to writing contemporary romance after deciding that life is too short not to have fun. She writes romantic comedy with an edge, and new adult books that push contemporary boundaries. From billionaires to BBWs to rock stars, Julia finds a sensual, goofy joy in every book she writes, but unlike Trevor from *Random Acts of Crazy*, she has never kissed a chicken.

She loves to hear from her readers by email at jkentauthor@gmail.com, on Twitter @jkentauthor, and on Facebook at
https://www.facebook.com/jkentauthor

Visit her blog at
http://jkentauthor.blogspot.com

Made in the USA
San Bernardino, CA
28 November 2014